The Olive Trees

Copyright © by Akin Yilmaz

ISBN 979 8 7466 7011 3

Dedicated to my father, Yilmaz Mehmet.

ONE

Terra, Cyprus, 330 BC

A shred of light prized opened the eyes of Zeno, but the moist sleep made it difficult for his eyes to fully open. Branches of an olive tree shielded his face from the basking sun as a voice echoed from the heavens.

'Are you alive?'

Was this the voice of God? A half-hearted attempt to get up proved fruitless, his body unable to respond to the instructions commended by his brain. Opening his eyes, a silhouette covered his face, but he could still make out a face hanging over him. Too ugly to be an angel he reached out.

'Are you one of the Gods?'

'No. I'm a simple farmer.'

The farmer dripped water onto the cracked lips of Zeno from his waterskin, gradually increasing the flow of water. Zeno grasped the waterskin and started to gulp down the water.

'Thank you,' Zeno said.

Zeno scanned the scene to establish his whereabouts. Olive trees, all he could see was row upon row of olive trees.

'Do these trees belong to you?' he asked the farmer.

'Yes, I produce olive oil.'

The farmer noticed that Zeno's white tunic was blood soaked with brown metallic stains.

'Where are you from?' asked the farmer.

'Tamassos.'

'I've heard of Tamassos, they mine for copper there,' Zeno confirmed by nodding his head.

While the farmer helped Zeno to his feet, he noticed that the back of his tunic was ripped, probably caused by a sharp jagged edged object. Zeno was unsteady on his feet leaning on the farmer for support.

'I do not mean to be personal, but how did you sustain your injuries?' questioned the farmer.

'My name is Zeno and I am, no, I was a slave and worked in the mines.'

'You say you were a slave. Are you a free man now?' Zeno grasped the farmer's hand.

'Yes, I'm a free man now.'

A palatial home appeared from behind the olive trees. Zeno hobbling along with the assistance of the farmer looked perplexed. How could a mere farmer live in home like this? The entrance of the home had a courtyard and, in the middle, appeared to be a well. A goat meandered along the yard followed by a couple of hens stalking him. The goat peered over and into the well but thought otherwise, mosquitoes were buzzing around the well. Clay pots lay strewn on the ground still wet from been washed. As Zeno and the farmer approached the house the pair were greeted by the sight of a woman standing in the doorway. Zeno rubbed his eye; his view obscured by the particles of dirt and the bright sunlight. The more he rubbed his eyes the more beautiful the woman became.

'This is my wife, Nefeli.'

Zeno touched her soft milky hand a contrast to his grimy callous hands. He turned to the farmer.

'My friend, I do not know your name.'

'Nikos.'

'This is our new friend Zeno,' Nikos said to Nefeli.
'Come in, Zeno,' Nefeli said with a smile.
The couple helped Zeno enter their home.
'Where are you from Zeno?' asked Nefeli.
'He is from Tamassos,' Nikos answered.
Nefeli stared at their new friend. Noticing the blood dirt-stained tunic and his greasy long hair and unkempt beard. His worn sandals seemed to be welded onto his feet with a concoction of blood and earth.
'You must be hungry?' commented Nefeli.
Zeno nodded thinking how obvious that must be. She disappeared out of the room followed by Nikos. Zeno wondered again how an olive farmer could live in such an opulent home. Maybe olives seemed to be the future rather than mining for copper, a thousand thoughts crossed his mind.
Nikos and Nefeli re-entered the room while whispering to themselves.
'I have to tend to my olive groves. My wife will tend to you and you are welcome to spend the night.'
Zeno was amazed at such hospitality.
'No, once I have rested, I will make my way. I can not impose on you this way,' Zeno said.
'Where will you go?' asked Nefeli.
'I have heard there is a fishing village on the coast. I am sure help is always wanted.'
'You can go tomorrow. Stay with us tonight, clean yourself, have a hearty meal and a good night's sleep,' Nikos pleaded.
After a brief minutes thought, Zeno accepted their offer.
'Thank you.'
'If you don't mind me telling you the first thing you need is a bath,' Nefeli said with such honesty.
'I have left you a towel and a clean tunic.'

Nikos left as Zeno was guided to the bathing room by Nefeli. Two large vases lay next to the stone slab. 'This vase contains cold water and the larger one has hot water,' She said pointing to them. 'You can use the block of clay. Would you like me to cut your hair and shave your beard?' she asked. 'It's been a long time since I have had both done, but I would like that.' He looked into her eyes and smiled. After Zeno washed himself, the first-time hot water had touched his skin in months, Nefeli cut his long coarse hair and applied a handful of olive oil to it. She used a sharp copper blade to shave his beard. Zeno closed his eyes his body so relaxed and tranquil that within a few minutes he fell asleep on the slab. Nefeli rubbed oil into his now smooth face and his hand, around the broken skin of his knuckles. She also noticed scars on the side of his body and more old lacerations on his back and on the soles of his feet. How could anyone inflict this type of sustained physical abuse on a fellow human being? Was this how all slaves were being treated in Tamassos Nefeli thought to herself?

Nikos came home to find Nefeli and Zeno sat around the dining table.

'Who is this strange man in our home?' asked Nikos.

'Do I look like a different man?' asked Zeno cheerfully.

'You are a handsome man my friend.'

Nefeli looked down and giggled in an embarrassed way as Zeno gave her a coy sideward glance. Nikos sat down next to his wife.

'It is not often we have guests for dinner. I would normally put some lamb on the fire, but tonight we have beans, bread and are own olives.'

Nikos broke some warm bread and dipped it into the plate of olives, staring at Zeno's new look.

'Look how good he looks,' Nikos commented nudging his wife.

'Eat your dinner,' Nefeli bashfully retorted.

Zeno ate his plate of beans in no time at all and helped himself to another plateful. Nefeli offered him some more bread which he gladly accepted.

'How did you get those scars on your body?' Nefeli enquired.

Zeno hesitated for a moment.

'In Tamassos you had to work from dawn to dusk. The favourite workers would get two or three breaks during the day. Men like me, would get one break for bread and water. If you disobeyed any orders the mine guards would beat you, beat you into submission. I was a leader of one of the work units so if any man in my unit was slack or was ill, as well as them getting beat I would also receive punishment. There was one day when an illness overcame my unit, and ten men were confined to camp. I was blamed.'

Nikos and Nefeli listened intently.

'One day my unit had a productive day we mined over twenty medimnos of copper. I was told that was the most produced in one day. Our reward was a feast for the whole unit. Lamb and chicken to eat and wine, vases of wine. We ate and drank until the early hours, some of the men drank so much they passed out. Dawn arrived but I was the only man at the mine on time. The guards told me to wait by the mine as they marched to the camp. I remember the evil appearing in the eye of the chief guard and knew the men would receive a god's beating. Only one guard was left to mind me. I heard a voice from above saying a word that entered my head and I then started to repeat it over and over again. The guard came closer and closer to hear the word.'

'What was the word?' Nefeli asked.

'Freedom.'

The gods were instructing me, and the will of my soul made me lash out and after a struggle with the guard I overpowered him and ran off. I spent six days and nights in the Troodos mountains living off the water from the mountain streams and wild fruits. My one saving grace was the shelter from the trees, they probably saved me from the sun.'

'Did any of the guards come looking for you?' asked Nikos.

'No. I do not think they would waste their time on one slave. A few years ago, a group of around twenty slaves escaped and headed towards Salamis. The Tamassos guards captured them and executed the group leaders. Escaping through the plains would never work as it is impossible to evade pursuers, but you will never be found in the mountains.'

Nikos and Nefeli looked at each other.

'Nefeli and I have been talking and the olive season has begun, so normally I would hire someone to help pick them and press them. If we pay you a gold stater for every week you work would you stay here?'

Zeno was shocked by their proposal.

'You would pay me?' questioned Zeno in disbelief.

'Yes, you are no longer a slave, you can work like any other free man,' reaffirmed Nikos.

Zeno stood up and reached out his hand and Nikos shook it.

Zeno lay in bed. The most comfortable thing he had laid on for many a year. The bed was made of olive wood with bronze legs, and the flokati sheepskin was soft and warm. After years of nightmares, he wondered if the dreams he used to have when he was a child would now come back. Would he ever see visons of his mother and father with the gods ever again? His eyes closed in hope and within seconds they opened again. Zeno could hear a noise from the back of the house. Attempting to fall asleep he closed his eyes, but the noise gradually grew louder and louder to a point where it began to irritate him. Slowly he climbed out of the bed and made his way on the stone floor to the back being guided in the dark by the strange noise until he saw the flickering light coming from Nikos and Nefeli's bedroom. Discovering that the noise was in fact Nefeli moaning while she straddled Nikos. Zeno stared and in due course he became aroused by the couple especially Nefeli's voluptuous body. He took a sharp intake of breath and crept back to his room still aroused by the scene he had just witnessed. Before long he began his journey to the gods and entered the eternal happiness of watching his parents strolling in the fields hand in hand. A smile appeared on his peaceful face. The light continued to flicker in Nikos and Nefeli's bedroom casting light over their naked bodies. Nefeli stroked his long hair and his beard.

'Do you like me with long hair and a beard?'

'I love them,' she replied.

'Why did you cut Zeno's hair and shave his beard?'

'I do not want anyone else to look like my husband.'

Zeno found her answer curious.

'Is that because you might be tempted by another man?'

'Never. I do not want any other man to look like you. Zeno is ugly without his beard.'

'Ugly, no, he is a handsome human specimen,' he retorted.

'My eyes are only for you; my body is only for you and my soul is only for you.'

'I have no doubt of that,' Nikos said as he leaned over and blew out the candle.

Harvesting the olives was labour intensive and time consuming. The trees were planted in dedicated areas, rows and rows that were long-lived and drought resistant, olive trees were a handily low maintenance form of farming. Nikos planted his trees amongst fruit trees and his herd of goats, this was good practice as it was an easy way to keep groves weed free. The fruit trees provided some income in case the olive crop failed. Nikos showed Zeno the art of picking olives, a rapid hand motion that collected a handful rather than picking them one by one. These olives were to be used to produce oil therefore it did not matter if they were bruised or fell to the ground, all could be used and put into woven baskets. To reach the tallest branches of the tree a person required cat like agility and tough-skinned hands, durable enough to withstand the sharp twigs. Nikos had already filled a whole basket by the time Zeno had climbed to the top branches of his olive tree.

'How do you pick them with such speed?' a perplexed Zeno asked.

'Experience,' shouted Nikos.

It was early autumn and that meant the temperatures had begun to fall and the cool air from the Troodos mountains blew towards the village making the early mornings and evenings bearable and manageable for Nikos and Nefeli and the other villagers. Nevertheless, after a couple of hours of picking olives Zeno was wiping the sweat off his forehead. He lifted his third basket full of olives onto the other two, but he glanced over in envy to Nikos' baskets that numbered seven. Zeno was surprised to see Nefeli standing behind him holding a basket containing warm bread and goats' cheese. He made his way straight to the vase of water to quench his thirst.

'Nikos,' shouted Zeno.

Nikos waived in acknowledgement as he climbed down from one of the trees a few hundred yards away.

'This is good,' Zeno said tucking into the bread.

Nefeli parted one of the pieces of bread in half and inserted the goats' cheese in between the two halves.

'Try it this way,' she said handing Zeno the bread.

She laid a blanket onto the ground and they both lay down. Nikos was preoccupied with a goat that had become separated from its herd and was attempting to guide it back. Nefeli laughed at the situation.

'The goats always give him the run around. I don't understand but they only listen to me.'

'I can understand,' mumbled Zeno with his mouth full.

'What can you understand?' she questioned.

'I understand why all creatures, human and non, would listen to you. I do not know how to express it but you have a certain tone, a certain enchantment, more a goddess than human. I can also understand how my friend Nikos could fall in love you. I apologise.'

'Why do you apologise?' Nefeli asked.

'I'm not an educated man so I can not express myself in words and sometimes I find this frustrating. I would love to be able to write a poem, be able to play a musical instrument, be able to make political debate,' he said in an emotional voice.

'Would you mind if a woman taught you all these?'

'No, but which woman could teach me?'

'Me.'

'Did you go to school?' asked Zeno.

'No, girls do not go to school, but my mother taught me everything at home. She taught me to play the flute, I learned the poetry of Homer and studied science and languages.'

Zeno was taken back by her wealth of knowledge.

'Was your mother a scholar?' he asked.

'My mother was the sister of Pnytagoras, King of Salamis.'

That revelation nearly made Zeno choke on the bread. He pointed at her while he swallowed the contents in his mouth.

'Then by my feeble calculation you must be related to the current King of Salamis.'

Nefeli laughed.

'Yes, your feeble calculation is correct King Nicocreon is my first cousin. His father was my uncle,' Nefeli confirmed.

'Pnytagoras was given Tamassos by Alexander of Macedon,' Zeno interrupted.

'For a common slave you have good knowledge. Maybe you are not a common slave?' she mischievously commented.

'If only I was not a common slave that would be my dream. I have one question, if the King is your cousin why are you not living in Salamis?'

'I am lucky enough to have a choice, most people like yourself do not have any choices in life and my choice was to leave Salamis,' she explained.

'How did you meet Nikos?' he asked curiously.

'Nikos worked in the royal palace and was responsible for the kitchen. The King had a lavish dinner for the city elders, and I was assigned to supervise in the kitchens. Nikos burnt his hand on a hot pot and I attended to him. Over the next few days we spent time together and fell in love. It would have been impossible for us to live in the palace or even in the city. I spoke to the King about leaving Salamis and I was dreading that he would not approve of us, but he was most amenable. He suggested a land the other side of the Troodos mountains that was given to his father by the King of Marion as a tribute, a fertile land served by a year-round spring. The day of our departure the King gave us a gift, one hundred gold coins, Nikos and I used part of the gift to build our home and plant the olive trees. That was some years ago, time has gone so fast I cannot even remember the number of years.'

She handed him another piece of bread with cheese in between,

'Where are you from Zeno?'

'The Kingdom of Kyrenia. My mother was a slave to one of the merchants. I never knew my father. Well, my mother never told me who he was, but I suspect he was the merchant,' he explained.

'How did you end up in Tamassos?'

'I have always been good with my hands, working on the roads in Kyrenia made them tough, but the work was too hard. Breaking and lifting rocks took a toll on my body. In fact, the main reason for leaving Kyrenia was a dispute I had with one of the other slave leaders. No option apart from leaving was given to me so I was sent to Tamassos.'

'I washed your tunic' she said pointing to it hanging on a tree near the house. 'A very well-made tunic. I never saw any slave wear a tunic, especially one of this quality.'

'All slave leaders at Tamassos were given these tunics' replied Zeno.

Nefeli nodded in a way suggesting she was unconvinced by his answer.

Nikos came striding towards them.

'This must be a special occasion' Nikos said in a raised voice.

'Why?' quizzed Nefeli.

'My wife never usually brings me a lunch.'

'Yes, I do,' retorted Nefeli jumping up and poking Nikos in the ribs.

'I re-state my comment, you do but very rarely. This occasion must be to honour our guest and that I approve of,' Nikos said in a bowing motion.

Zeno gulped down some water and stood up.

'Nikos and Nefeli, my new friends I thank you both for the hospitality you have offered me. I know most people would have turned a blind eye towards me and sent me on my way, but you both took me in and for that human gesture I will repay you. I think I have more olives to pick.'

With that he went back to the olive tree and continued picking as Nikos and Nefeli laid on the blanket. Nikos poured water onto his dirty hands and rubbed them on the blanket.

'I like him, he is a good man,' he proclaimed.

'He is that,' reaffirmed Nefeli whilst she stared at Zeno climbing up the olive tree. In her mind she was not convinced about his story and that he was a slave, but still, there was something quite fascinating about him.

The lunch invigorated Zeno and while Nikos and Nefeli carried on with their lunch he picked every olive on the tree and filled his fourth basket, still three less than Nikos had filled. Competition had always been part of Zeno's life and this was no exception, he was determined to pick more olives than Nikos. Before Nikos had finished his lunch and kissed Nefeli, Zeno had filled a further two baskets leaving him just one behind. His hands began to show the signs of a hard days graft, a kaleidoscope of colours amalgamating the black dirt of the tree, the red blood from the cuts and the green and yellow stains of the olives.

'You are doing well my friend,' Nikos shouted out.

'Normally no one can keep up with me and harvest the same number as me,' he continued.

'I have one question. Why do you harvest them so early? If you left them one or two months more, they will be riper and produce more oil' Zeno asked.

'The earlier they are harvested and pressed, the finer the oil, but you are right leaving collection later in the season allows the olives to ripen more, turn black and thus more oil can be pressed from them. Olive oil is like wine in that different qualities exist. Pressing when they are green produces the best quality that is edible, the oil produced when they are black can be used to burn in lamps, cleaning and to massage the body and medicine' Nikos explained.

'Who do you sell the oil to?'

'Merchants in Marion. They then sell and distribute all through the Kingdom. The finer oil is more expensive than the later oil, but I still sell more of the finer than the other. Come on my friend we still have more to harvest,' beckoned Nikos.

The baskets began to stack up and as olives produce a full harvest only every other year this year was a bumper crop. The autumn afternoon was hot but bearable compared with the summer months. A fresh breeze blew down stream airing the valley of olive groves. Zeno counted the number of full baskets; he had amassed a total of sixteen. Strolling over to Nikos he counted his baskets and remarkably Nikos had also filled sixteen baskets.

'We are even,' proclaimed Zeno.

Nikos walked towards him with a serious scowl on his face, he stopped and offered his hand, Zeno shook his hand and both men smiled.

'I have met my match,' admitted Nikos.

The pair made their way down to the stream and Zeno kicked off his sandals and jumped into the stream, the cold water felt soothing on his feet and legs. Nikos washed his hands and face.

'Come on my friend, we have a couple of hours of sunlight left. On my best day I harvested twenty baskets. I have dreamt that one day I will beat it, today is the day to fulfil that dream,' said a buoyant Nikos beckoning Zeno.

'Let us go,' shouted Zeno jumping out of the stream.

The pair walked side by side gradually increasing the length of their stride as they approached the olive groves.

'Why do you and Nefeli have no slaves?' Zeno asked.

'If I had my choice, I would have slaves, you have seen the effort needed to harvest the olives. This is the easy part of the process, wait until we have to press them and produce the oil.'

'I take that to mean the final choice not to have slaves belongs to Nefeli.'

Nikos turned his head to Zeno.

'My wife believes no human being should be a slave.'

'I agree with her,' Zeno said with a nod.

'Nefeli, is cousin to the King of Salamis,' Nikos said.

'Yes, she told me earlier how you both met and fell in love at the palace. It must have been difficult for you to leave your family in Salamis?' Zeno asked.

'Oh, did she not tell you why we left?'

'Yes, she said you could not stay in Salamis and the King gave you both the land here' confirmed Zeno.

Nikos shook his head.

'That is not entirely the truth. We were banished from Salamis by the King.'

'Banished!' Zeno said aghast.

'Nicrocoen did not approve of our relationship, he believed that Nefeli should not marry a common citizen like me. At first, we were worried that he would put us on a ship to the land of the Egyptians. Nefeli was one of the

King's favourite cousins, hence his decision to give us this land. The state declaration proclaimed that we would be banished from Salamis for ever and we would never be allowed to set foot there again. The gods have looked after us and given as a fertile land and we have prospered,' explained Nikos.

'Your soul must yearn to return back to see your family?' asked Zeno.

'Yes, both my soul and heart ache as this is against human nature and human instinct, but I know one day I will return to Salamis,' Nikos said with passion.

'Hopefully, my friend, hopefully,' Zeno said putting his hand on Nikos' shoulder.

Darkness descended and Nefeli had prepared a feast for the two men. The centrepiece was one of her favourite dishes, bean and spinach stew topped with garlic and onions. This was accompanied with freshly baked bread, olives, and goat's cheese. A tray of figs and pears rounded off the meal. An amphora jug of black wine with two kylix drinking cups awaited the men's return. She surveyed the room with a great sense of pride as Nikos and Zeno entered triumphantly.

'All hail the record breakers,' Nikos proclaimed.

Nefeli poured the wine into the cups and handed them to the pair.

'How many baskets did you harvest?' She enquired.

Nikos downed the wine in one gulp while Zeno was slightly more measured.

'I picked twenty two baskets, but my friend here managed to fill twenty three baskets,' Nikos exclaimed pointing at Zeno while pouring himself another cup of wine.

'Twenty three baskets, you must have broken your back?' Nefeli said.

Zeno lifted his hands to show her the extent of the bruising and his swollen fingers.

'Come and I will bathe those hands' she said beckoning Zeno over.

She put his damaged hands into a bowl of cold water. The relief was evident on his face.

'Keep them in the water,' she told him.

She fetched a vase of warm olive oil and a towel, lifting Zeno's hands out of the water she dried them before rubbing in the olive oil.

'Keep the oil on them.'

'Thank you for this and also for looking after me,' Zeno said staring directly into her emerald green eyes. His slightly darker, olive coloured eyes complemented hers as both set of eyes met in the middle.

'More wine?'

The fixed gaze was interrupted by Nikos, holding an empty jug of wine.

'I did not dilute the wine,' Nefeli confessed.

In normal practice she would dilute the wine with five parts water to two parts wine as black wine had a potent effect. Zeno stood up and held her arm.

'Do not dilute it, let Nikos enjoy the evening,'

She nodded in agreement.

Zeno tucked into the stew but was most fond of dipping the bread into the olive oil. Nikos was still drinking and placed his hand around Zeno's shoulder.

'Tomorrow my friend we press the olives to produce the oil. Dawn awakening.'

'I will be up,' Zeno firmly said in a way to make it understood that it would be Nikos who would struggle to get up in the morning.

'Good, I will see you then,' Nikos blurted out as he stumbled towards his bedroom.

Nefeli began to clear the table.

'Do not worry I will clean up. Go and join your husband,' Zeno said pointing towards the bedroom.

'No, I must tidy and clean,' Nefeli stated.

'You are not a slave,' proclaimed Zeno.

The pair stared at each other, a repeat of the gaze from earlier on.

'I wish you a goodnight Zeno.'

With that farewell she made her way towards the bedroom. The long day had taken its toll on Zeno's hands and he was finding great difficulty with the dexterity of holding more than a couple of objects in his hands, but somehow, he cleared the table and began to wash the dishes. He disposed of the waste food in a bucket before taking it outside to pour into the trough for the goats and hens. He even found time to sweep up and by the time he was finished the kitchen and dining area were glistening. Retiring to bed he expected to close his eyes and fall asleep immediately but sometimes things don't turn out as expected. Like the previous night, a certain noise was coming from the back bedroom and like the previous night temptation got the better of him. Tiptoeing through the house the noise grew louder and louder as he came the open doorway of the couple's bedroom but the noise was quite unexpected, Nikos lay on his back snoring like a herd of bulls. Nefeli lay naked next to him with her hand between her legs. She turned to see Zeno's shadow. Zeno stepped into the bedroom and they began staring at each other intensely, all the while Nefeli's hand was moving more and more vigorously. Zeno was motionless and mesmerized as he engaged in this act of voyeurism as Nefeli's groaning grew stronger and stronger and all but drowned out the persistence snoring coming from Nikos.

Nefeli reached her crescendo and nonchalantly gave Zeno a smile when she saw through his tunic that he was fully aroused before turning over. Zeno could not bear it and walked outside to calm his body down and hearing the sound of the stream he began to run towards it and leapt into it without hesitation. The cold water initially made his body shiver but after a few moments he submerged his whole body. Climbing out he lay by the streams edge viewing the stars and listening to the persistently noisy crickets, that in a funny kind of way sounded like a lullaby putting Zeno to sleep.

Nikos emerged from the house in the same tunic that he wore the previous day, stains of black wine and stew gave the dull grey tunic a more abstract feel, add to this his long hair and bushy beard and it gave him an almost unkempt appearance. Through his bleary strawberry tinted eyes, he could just about make out the muscular figure of Zeno waiting by the stacked baskets of olives. Zeno gave him a wry smile as he approached him.
'I thought you said dawn?' Zeno said with a large slice of sarcasm.
'Come on my friend I will show you how to produce the oil,' Nikos mumbled as he ignored Zeno's quip.
Nikos led Zeno to one of the huts in the compound. In the middle of the hut stood a large stone vat held up by eight wooden stilts. A tap was attached at the base of the stone vat. Six wooden steps led up to the vat. Nikos went outside lifted one of the baskets of olives and marched back in, negotiated the steps and poured the olives into the vat and looked at Zeno. Nikos acknowledged the demonstration and accepted the challenge by rushing outside lifting a basket onto his shoulder and rushed back in and almost stumbled on the steps before hurling the olives into the vat. Nikos smiled; it was going to be a

strength sapping morning. They poured a quarter of the olives into a large vat. Two pairs of large wooden sandals lay next to the vat. Nikos put one pair on and beckoned Zeno to put the other pair on. Nikos climbed into the vat and started crushing the olives underfoot, Zeno followed suit. The olives slowly turned to mush while the oil rose to the top.

'Every olive has to be crushed,' Nikos said loudly.

The oil splatted all over the men's legs and the lower half of their tunics. The tap was then turned on and the initial oil was funneled into large vases. The remaining pulp was placed into woven bags, and the bags themselves were pressed. Hot water was poured over the pressed bags to wash out the remaining oil, and the dregs of the pulp was washed away. The day was long, and Zeno wondered how one or even two men could manage it all. Producing the oil would take several days, but the rewards for selling olive oil were huge and he realised that if the process were managed more efficiently and in a timelier manner great wealth could be derived from this land.

Soon it was afternoon and the two men emerged from the hut after almost seven hours pressing olives, both soaked below their waistlines in olive oil.

'I am going to the stream to wash,' Zeno informed Nikos.

'I'll ask Nefeli to prepare some food for us,' Nikos replied as he walked towards the house.

The autumn sunshine was intense, and Zeno had to shield his eyes with his hand as he ambled down the path to the stream. He waded into the stream, but it felt too cold to swim in it and the current seemed strong today. Climbing out he heard a sound echoing from downstream. Nervously he began to walk towards the sound, and it became clear that it was the sound of voices. He kept walking but he could no longer hear the voices. Trying to focus his eyes he saw a movement through the trees and as he got nearer, he could see a horse grazing by a tree. On the horse's saddle was a shield, this made him panic. He turned back but standing there were three soldiers. His body froze. All three soldiers were wearing metal breastplates and ankle plates, two of them were hoplite foot soldiers holding spears while the soldier in the middle, the Captain, had a short sword tied around his waist.

'What is your name my friend?' asked the Captain.

Zeno paused for a moment.

'I am Nikos,' he said.

The Captain turned to one of the soldiers.

'Do you recognize him?'

The soldier stared at Zeno, for what seemed like an eternity.

'No, the man we want had a beard and long hair' he replied.

'Who are you looking for?' Zeno nervously asked.

'A foot soldier from Tamassos who murdered his regiment Colonel and two other soldiers. He is known as Zeno,' the Captain confirmed.

'Do you live here?' the Captain enquired.

'Yes, this is my land. I live in the house further up from the stream. I produce olive oil.' Zeno had to think on his feet.

'Have you seen any strangers in the past few days?' the Captain continued his questioning.

'Yes, someone has been helping me harvest the olives the last couple of days. He is from Tamassos and his name is Zeno.'

'Where is he now?' the Captain asked.

'He is at the house,' Zeno said pointing.

The Captain gave a hand gesture to the soldiers and they started walking towards the house. Zeno tentatively stepped backwards and slowly started to walk in the other direction, but the Captain turned towards him.

'Where are you going?'

Zeno stopped in his tracks.

'I need to continue harvesting the olive trees,' Zeno said pensively.

'No. you are coming with us, you lead the way,' said the stern Captain.

Zeno led the soldiers to the house whilst trying to formulate some form of a plan in his head to escape this desperate situation. But just as several thoughts crossed his mind the situation worsened as in the distance, he could see Nikos walking directly towards them. Zeno suddenly stopped prompting the soldiers to also do so. The Captain starred at Nikos as he got closer.

'He is Zeno,' shouted Zeno pointing at Nikos.

At that precise moment, a stiff breeze blew from the stream blowing Nikos' long hair in all directions. The Captain turned to one of soldiers.

'Is that him?'

'Yes, I am sure that is him,' confirmed the soldier.

'He can be very aggressive,' Zeno threw in.

'Come on,' the Captain said marching forward placing his right hand on top of the handle of his sword.

Nikos approached them.

'Are you Zeno of Tamassos?'shouted the Captain.

A state of confusion was etched on Nikos' face.

'No, he is Zeno,' Nikos said pointing at Zeno.

'He lies. I found him under an olive tree two days ago and me and my wife welcomed him into our home,' Zeno quickly retorted.

'How can you believe him. I am Nikos and this is my land. He said he was a slave from the mines of Tamassos and me and my wife took him in,' pleaded Nikos. The soldiers were completely confused by the whole situation. The Captain was in disbelief poking one of the soldiers in the ribs.

'Which one is he?' demanded the Captain.

'I don't know. I only saw him a couple of times. All I can remember is that he had long hair and a beard. The soldier said in a defensive way.

'Stop,' shouted Nikos.

'Tie them both up,' ordered the Captain.

Using rope kept under their breastplates the soldiers tied the hands of both Zeno and Nikos.

'My wife will identify me,' Nikos shouted.

'Lead us to the house,' ordered the Captain.

Nikos was in a hurry, whilst Zeno was hesitant prompting the Captain to push him along.

'What is the name of your wife?' The Captain asked Zeno.

'Nefeli. She is the cousin of King Nicocreon of Salamis'

'A king's cousin,' repeated the Captain.

The view of the house made Nikos walk faster, but one of the soldiers held him back.

'I cannot imagine a King's Cousin marrying either one of you men,' the Captain sarcastically commented.

The men entered the courtyard.

'Nefeli,' shouted Zeno at the top of his voice.

This incensed Nikos and he charged at Zeno, shoulder charging him to the ground. The soldiers restrained Nikos and helped Zeno to his feet.

'Hold them here,' the Captain instructed the soldiers.

With a purposeful stride the Captain entered the house.

'Hello,' he shouted out.

Nefeli rushed in.

'I am a Captain from Tamassos. There are two men outside one is your husband and the other a man called Zeno, who is from Tamassos. Can you come with me and point to your husband?'

A state of anguish engraved her face.

'My Lady, would you follow me?'

Nefeli hesitated for a moment and reluctantly followed the Captain outside. The soldiers held Zeno and Nikos in line a few yards apart. The Captain and Nefeli walked side by side towards the men.

'When I stop, I want you to point to your husband,' he whispered.

The Captain stopped and turned to her.

Nikos stared at her intensely. Zeno awaited the inevitable.

A tear trickled down Nefeli's face.

'Point to your husband' the Captain insisted.

Nefeli gently raised her hand and pointed at Zeno.

'What are you doing?' screamed out Nikos.

Zeno looked at Nefeli in astonishment. The Captain also had a puzzled expression on his face. He moved forward and put his hand on Zeno's right shoulder.

'This man is your husband?' the Captain shouted out.

'Yes!' shouted back Nefeli.

Nikos rushed over and grabbed Nefeli's dress with his tied hands.

'What are you doing? Why are saying he is your husband?' he shouted.

The two soldiers pulled Nikos away as Nefeli stood motionless and closed her eyes. The Captain stood face to face and untied Zeno's hands.

'The gods have foretold. They have given you an abundance of luck but be careful once the gods start to ignore you your luck will run out. Maybe one day we will meet again my friend,' the Captain uttered to Zeno.

The soldiers were struggling to restrain Nikos. The Captain rushed towards him and punched Nikos in the stomach which doubled him up falling onto his knees, tears streamed down his face.

'Please believe me my name is Nikos and I am from Salamis. I beg you to believe me,'

'Tie his hands behind his back,' instructed the Captain.

'I cannot believe you, the Lady chose her husband, so you are Zeno from Tamassos and we are instructed by the City Council to take you back there,' the Captain explained.

'She is my wife,' Nikos screamed at the top of his voice.

The soldiers lifted him up and held him by each arm.

'Let us go,' the Captain said marching onwards.

Nikos turned to look at Nefeli.

'Why?' he shouted. 'Why?'

One of the soldiers forcibly turned his head back and they pulled him along.

'What are you going to do to me?' Nikos asked in total anguish.

'We are taking you back to Tamassos where you will stand trial. If the council find you guilty you will be executed,' the Captain said in a matter-of-fact way.

'But I am not Zeno,' Nikos shouted.

'The council will decide,' the Captain replied.

'If you take me to Salamis the King will vouch for me,' pleaded Nikos.

'No, we are not going to Salamis,' the Captain adamantly said.

'But you can not execute me, I am not Zeno. You have the wrong man,' Nikos continued to plead.

They reached the horse and the soldiers tied Nikos' hands to a lead attached to the saddle of the horse. The Captain untied and then mounted the horse and rode on pulling

Nikos with him, whilst the two soldiers walked either side of the grief-stricken Nikos.

Zeno stood in front of Nefeli still trying to digest the ramifications of her actions. He wiped away her tears with his fingers. The two stared at each other as Nikos' distraught voice echoed through the land.

'Why did you tell the soldiers that I was Nikos?' Zeno asked.

Nefeli shook her head as in disbelief of what she had just done.

'Something within my soul made me say it. I cannot explain,' Nefeli said still in tears.

Zeno firmly grabbed her hand.

'I know what you have said has saved me, but if they take Nikos away you will probably never see him again. I only told the soldiers that I was Nikos so it could give me time to escape them. I did not envisage them taking him. It is not too late; go and tell the soldiers the truth and I will leave.

Just tell them you were scared and did not know what you were saying,' said Zeno.

She shook her head.

'He is your husband do you not love him?' Zeno said angrily.

'The gods have foretold Nikos' fate. I can not alter that fate. They have also foretold your fate and your destiny is to stay here with me,' she said.

Zeno could not understand Nefeli's words. He kept looking back expecting the soldiers to come back any minute and say this was a giant misunderstanding.

'Do you want me to stay here, stay here with you, act like your husband?' he asked.

'Yes, I want you to be my husband in every respect.'

Zeno's heart was pounding out of his chest, confused, and even frightened at the events that had just unfolded. Nefeli took his hand.

'Come let's go inside,' she said nonchalantly.

Zeno hesitated. He looked back in the direction of Nikos and the soldiers and then turned back to Nefeli.

'You say my destiny is to stay here with you. I will become Nikos?' he questioned.

'You are Nikos,' she said.

They both walked into the house. All was silent except for the breeze blowing through the branches of the olive trees.

TWO

Terra, 122 AD

Sweat poured down the side of the Roman soldier's galea helmet, considering it was the height of summer in Cyprus this was an inevitable consequence. Matters were not helped by the fact that the soldier was standing on top of the observation tower at the army castrum just outside the village with the midday sun rapidly approaching. In the distance the port of Arsinoe was visible and the glistening sea of the Mediterranean beyond. On the opposite side lay the outline of the Troodos mountains with the peak of Mount Olympus standing out in the middle of the range. The soldier squinted as he could barely make out movement on the mountain path approach to the camp. Visibility in his left eye was poor due to the damaged inflicted to it during the suppressing of the Jewish uprising in Salamis some six years earlier. The movement turned out to be a convoy of horse drawn carts led by four soldiers on horseback. The Soldier on the tower counted six carts with his good eye before ringing the bell.

The camp Prefect, Titus Antonius, rushed out of his quarters.

'Prepare to greet him,' he shouted.

One of the gate guards nudged his colleague.

'Who are we greeting?' questioned the guard.

'Legatus Augusti pro praetore' his colleague said in a panic.

'Open the gate,' shouted Titus.

The gate of the camp opened and some minutes later the convoy entered under the arch of the gate and into the camp. Titus stood in the middle of the courtyard flanked by two legionaries on either side of him. The Legatus Augusti pro praetore was the military governor of Cyprus who was stationed at Salamis. He approached Titus before dismounting.

'I am Lucius Octavis' he pronounced.

'Hail Lucius Octavis, it is my honour to meet you' said Titus raising his arm. 'Please follow me, it would be my pleasure to offer you some sustenance after such a long and arduous journey.'

'Could you offer the same hospitality to my men and tend to the horses,' requested Lucius.

'Certainly,' said Titus as he led Lucius into a room with a large lectus with two smaller couches on either side and a round ornate table in the middle. Copious quantities of food covered the table, bread, figs, grapes, olives, and fish to name just a few things. A male servant brought in a large vase.

'Would you like some wine?' the servant enviously asked.

'No, I do not drink wine, water is fine with me,' Lucius said.

'Titus sit. What news do you have for me?' asked Lucius.

Titus sat on the smaller lectus taking off his helmet.

'I have to be honest with you Lucius, it has been very quiet in this region. Every three months I venture down to Arsinoe to collect taxes from the port,' Titus explained.

'Yes, while I am here, I would like to see the camps tax records, but that is not the only reason I am here. My tenure as Governor comes to an end soon and I wanted to visit all the major cities on the Island before I left so I can brief my successor,' Lucius explained.

'Where will you go when you leave Cyprus?' Titus asked.

'The emperor is building a wall in Britannia, and he has chosen me to travel with him and assist with supervising the build,'

'Britannia, another island,' Titus said with a smile.

'The army is experiencing problems with the local tribes there and this wall will act as a defense barrier against these tribes. It will stretch across the island and require thousands of men to build it, so it will be a challenge,' Lucius said.

'Speaking to a soldier who served there he told me the people of Britannia are barbarians and uncivilised, the gods served them well when the empire invaded there,' Titus said.

'Yes, I will take more weaponry there as it will be a more hostile territory than here,' Lucius said.

'Is it the truth that the climate is cold and wet?' asked a curious Titus.

'Yes, I hear that is the truth.'

'Take some lambs wool from here,' Titus said.

'I also carry a statue of our Emperor Hadrian that I want erected by the port in Arsinoe. Tomorrow you will escort me to Arsinoe and recommend the best position for the statue. You are probably wondering why I have travelled with these many carts. I hear there is an olive grove near here that produces the best olive oil in Cyprus. Is this true?' he asked Titus.

'Yes, Lucius. I know the landowner,' said Titus.

'Good, I want to take back as many vases of oil that I can fit on the carts. Can you take me to him this afternoon?' Lucius asked.

'Certainly. Please have something to eat and I will escort you to my quarters so you can rest while I go and make all necessary arrangements. In this jar is the olive oil from the nearby grove,' Titus said pouring the oil into a small bowl.

Lucius broke off a portion of bread and dipped it into the olive oil. Titus waited while Lucius tasted it. 'I must agree this is the best oil I have tasted on the Island,' Lucius confirmed. 'We also heat the oil and use it to heal any wounds that any of the soldiers may have,' said Titus. 'Good, we will go there this afternoon,' Lucius instructed. Titus exited the room as fast as humanly possible with a concerned look sketched across his face. He rushed to the room where all the camps records were kept including the book that recorded all the taxes collected by him. Titus had a good understanding of figures and entered all amounts collected into the book himself. What he did not record was all amounts of tax he took for himself, hence the concerned look. After a few minutes of thought he closed the book and locked the room with the hope that the olive oil and statue of Hadrian would distract Lucius and time would run out for him to inspect the books.

The Olive groves were close to the camp and a path adjacent to a stream led to the olive farmer's house. Lucius and Titus were making their way towards the house their horses slowly meandering around the path too hot to worry about the bothersome flies. As they approached the house a boy who was playing outside saw them and ran into the house and a few seconds later the landowner came out. Lucius and Titus dismounted, and the boy ran to take their horses and tied them by the trough, the horses grateful for the water.

'Welcome,' said the landowner.

'Zygos, this is Lucius Octavis, Governor of Cyprus,' announced Titus.

'It is a blessing to have such an honourable person visit me,' Zygos said humbly.

Lucius shook his hand.

'I am a working man just like you,' Lucius replied. 'Please come let us sit in the shade,' Zygos said escorting the Romans to the veranda by the side of his house.

'I hear from good authority that the oil you produce from your olives is the best on the Island,' Lucius said.

'This land has been owned by my family for hundreds of years. I remember my grandfather telling me that olives have been grown here since the days of Alexander of Macedon,' Zygos informed them.

'Do you have any I can purchase from you?' asked Lucius.

'It is too early for this year's crop. The olives will not be ready for another month or two, but I do have oil from last year that I can sell you,' explained Zygos.

'I sampled some of your oil at the camp last night, if that is from the same yield, then yes I will take it,' Lucius said.

'How much would you require?' asked Zygos.

'I have six carts so how many vases of oil can you fit in them?' Lucius responded.

Zygos thought for a few seconds.

'I think you should be able to take back one hundred vases,' said Zygos.

'That is sixteen to seventeen per cart,' Lucius worked out in an instant leaving both Titus and Zygos impressed by his quick arithmetic.

'Do you have this amount?' Lucius asked Zygos.

'Come with me.' Zygos escorted the men to the large outbuilding at the back of the main house and opened the gate to reveal a vast number of vases.

'How many are there?' Lucius asked.

'Two hundred,' confirmed Zygos.

'This was produced last year?' asked Lucius.

'Yes, we produced six hundred vases worth, but I have sold most of it, some of it to the camp,' said Zygos.

Titus stared at Zygos nervously.

'Good, I will pay you four gold aureus for each vase, a total of four hundred aureus,' offered Lucius.

'Normally the price is five aureus for each vase, but since you are purchasing one hundred vases I agree to four per vase,' Zygos said with a smile. Lucius nodded and shook Zygos' hand.

'My men will come with the carts tomorrow morning to load up before we head back to Salamis, one of the soldiers will pay you the money,' Lucius said.

Lucius bid farewell to Zygos and by the time Titus had whispered a few words to Zygos, Lucius was already by the horses.

That night Titus put on a lavish banquet for Lucius and his men. The camp cellar had been emptied of its stock of wine and the long tables consisted of dozens of vases. Food was plentiful but the soldiers were only interested in drinking, they wanted to put a dent in the one hundred gallons of wine per year that most Roman soldiers consumed. Lucius had his own personal vase of water. Titus sat next to him and even though he drank wine he made sure he kept sober and made sure he kept an eye on Lucius.

'Titus, I want to inspect the tax records first thing in the morning before we set off to Arsinoe with the statue,' Lucius said in a loud voice in an attempt to get himself heard over the raucous noise in the hall.

'Certainly, Lucius, I will have them ready for you,' mumbled Titus.

Lucius stood up and in turn Titus stood up as an act of courtesy.

'I am going to retire for the night we have an early start tomorrow, let the men enjoy themselves, they will sleep well tonight,' Lucius said content that his men were happy.

'Would you like me to escort you to your quarters?'

'No, I remember the way.'

Once Lucius left, Titus was left to ponder on the situation he had found himself. His position as camp commander was under threat, depending on what justice would be dealt for defrauding the army, he could see himself being banished to the far reaches of the empire or a more extreme outcome if found guilty, summary execution. Titus remembered an incident when he served in Egypt when an officer was found guilty of theft the culprit was placed in a sack of poisonous snakes and thrown into the River Nile probably to become a feast for the crocodiles. Images of enormous snakes flooded the mind of Titus that night making it impossible for him to sleep and leaving him in a cold sweat for most of the night. One indelible image was seeing himself floating down a river unable to use any part of his numb body.

'Help!' He screamed out.

Eyes wide open he made the decision that he could no longer endure any further excruciating nightmares and took the decision to get up and prepare for the uncertainty he would face this day.

Weary looking soldiers began to emerge from the depths of the camp, it was evident that the nights festivities had taken its toll on this band of soldiers. The queue for the well was growing by the minute, the soldiers wanting to quench their thirst, an effect of an alcoholic laden evening. Titus stood statuesque in the middle of the courtyard his body armor glistening in the morning sun as the soldiers, some off balance, navigated themselves around his bulky frame all unaware that he had been awake for several hours. Lucius came bounding into the courtyard, a wry smile crossed his face once he saw the condition of his men.

'Load the statue,' he shouted at the group standing by Hadrian's statue.

The Soldiers covered the statue with a cloth and lifted it. Lucius watched as they precariously put it onto the cart. Titus stood motionless while staring at Lucius.

'Titus,' shouted Lucius.

Titus ignored him.

Lucius marched over to him.

'Titus mount up we go to Arsinoe.'

Winding up and down the narrow path the convoy of six men on horseback were followed by the horse and cart. Titus led the way followed by Lucius and four of his men. Titus turned to Lucius.

'Be careful these paths can give way. A few months ago, we lost two horses when the cart they were pulling fell down the hill.'

That piece of information made the two soldiers riding on the cart glance at each other nervously.

Arsinoe was a prosperous city that relied on the ships that arrived and departed from the port and the road leading down to the city was one of the most scenic on the island, it was the center of a great bay. As they arrived in the city Lucius rode up next to Titus.

'Take me to the harbour master. The statue should be erected at the center of the harbour.'

'I know the exact place,' replied Titus.

Titus escorted them to the entrance of the harbour and as they arrived the large wooden gate opened; four large merchant ships were anchored in the port. The harbour master stood to attention behind the gate. As they dismounted the harbour master approached Lucius.

'An honour to meet you, Lucius Octavis. I am Andreas, master of the harbour,' he said raising his hand and bowing his head.

'It was always my intention to visit Arsinoe. A beautiful bay and the land on this part of the Island is so fertile. I regret that I have not visited sooner. I have a Statue of the emperor that I want erected in the harbour,' Lucius explained.

Titus came bounding over pointing in the direction of the harbour masters building.

'The emperor can overlook the bay from next to the harbour building.' Titus suggested.

Lucius surveyed the area and walked towards the harbour's edge. The turquoise sea reflected off his body armour and onto the harbour wall. He then strolled towards the building and pointed to the ground. Titus nodded to confirm the exact spot.

'Excellent suggestion Titus. The emperor will stand here,' Lucius proclaimed. It needed the strength of three men to lift the plinth from the cart, the statue required six men. Andreas ordered his men to help the soldiers and an array of tools were used to prepare the ground for the plinth to sit before they secured the statue on it. Lucius and Andreas took a stroll by the waterfront while Titus followed a few steps behind.

'The consignment of copper from Tamassos should be arriving any day, so it is very important that it is loaded onto the ships as quickly as possible. I have received word that Rome requires more and more of the copper ore,' Lucius explained.

'My men are all experienced in loading and unloading cargo that will not be an issue. It may not be my position to say so stop me if you wish, we have tons and tons of copper here, but the problem is Rome do not have enough ships to transport the metal,' Andreas said.

'You speak the truth Andreas, Rome must build more ships this is evident, but all their resources are spent sustaining their army and expanding the empire. They demand more and more copper and olive oil but seem not to realise there is only a limited capacity we can send them. The sea is vast, and, in the future, whoever rules the sea will rule the known World. When I leave Cyprus, I hope I will be able to advise the emperor. I know he respects other people's opinions and ideas and he has made it a goal to travel to every part of the empire and beyond.' Lucius proudly said to Andreas.

'Lucius, I am a seafarer so for me the World revolves around the sea and my ambition one day would be to build a ship so large it could sail to the edge of the World,' Andreas said.

Lucius put his hand on Andreas' shoulder.

'If I live long enough, I would love to travel on this ship with you Andreas.'

Both men smiled as Lucius looked back at the men still in the process of erecting Hadrian's statue.

'Titus, tell them to hurry up. I do not have the time to wait around,' Lucius shouted.

Titus wandered over to the men not overly concerned about the time it was taking to put up the statue.

'The ground here is too hard,' complained one the soldiers.

'Carry on, carry on,' Titus nonchalantly said.

He ambled back to where Lucius was standing.

'Why are they taking so long?' Lucius asked Titus.

'They are finding great difficulty in planting the plinth as the ground is so hard.'

Lucius uncertain on what to do pondered for a minute or so.

'Titus, we are going back to the camp. When the men here are finished, they can make their own way back. We need to collect the olive oil before I return back to Salamis,' Lucius said.

'I will inform the men,' Titus replied.

Lucius turned back and put his hand up to gain the attention of Andreas, who came rushing over.

'I have to head back to the camp; the bay is a beautiful place and you are a great harbour master. Maybe one day we can sail to the other side of the World together,' Lucius said to Andreas.

'I wish the gods look after you Lucius,' Andreas replied.

The pair nodded in mutual admiration.

Lucius and Titus rode back to the camp together.

'Can you show me the tax records when we get back to the camp?' asked Lucius.

'I will take you straight to the room where all camp records are held,' Titus reluctantly said.

'Yes, I still have a long day ahead me.'

'Camp records are all up to date, I can not envisage it would take you too long to check Lucius.'

'All I want to see is the tax collected in the last year,' Lucius confirmed.

Silence marked the remainder of the journey back to the camp, but numerous loud thoughts entered their minds breaking the silence in their heads. Titus, justifiably, was concerned that Lucius would discover that he had been falsifying the records and pilfering monies for himself. Lucius timed things meticulously and wanted to arrive back to Salamis before nightfall, with the vases of olive oil and ensure that the statue of Hadrian was properly erected.

The camp gates opened to let in Lucius and Titus. The soldiers stood fully prepared aside the horses and carts. Lucius dismounted and walked over to them.

'Men, we shall leave soon to collect the olive oil,' Lucius said.

'Sir, to save time we can go and collect the oil,' One of his Captains responded back.

'No, I will come too,' Lucius insisted.

Titus headed towards the room that held the camp records. Lucius followed closely with an identical stride pattern. Titus took out a set of keys from his pocket and opened the iron gate of the room. A large window with iron bars ensured plenty of sunlight reached the table in the middle and the surrounding boxes of books.

'Take a seat, Lucius.'

Titus located a box and pulled out one of the record books, which consisted of about twenty pages of papyrus glued together in a long roll and opened it up on the table. The books were stored in boxes as insects liked eating papyrus.

'This is the record of all taxes collected in the last year,' Titus confirmed.

'Do you have a record of all camp paid purchases for the year?' Lucius asked.

Titus pulled out another book and placed it on the table. Titus sat on the opposite side of the table to Lucius who methodically checked every entry on the page line by line.

'Where do you store all the camps money?'

'In a basement store, exactly below this room,' Titus replied.

After a few minutes Lucius closed the book and pushed it aside.

'And the record of camp purchases?'

Titus pushed the book towards Lucius, who started reading each line from the top of the page. A trickle of sweat dripped down from Titus' brow.

'What is this figure?' Lucius said pointing to a number on the page and turning the book around to Titus.

'six hundred,' Titus said as Lucius quickly turned the book back, so Titus was unable to read the rest of the line. Lucius closed the book having spent even less time reviewing it than the tax record. Titus anxiously waited for a comment. Lucius stood up.

'Good, you can put them back, lock up and we need to go and collect the olive oil,' Lucius said marching out of the room. Titus, with great relief etched on his face, gladly placed the books back into their boxes.

By the time Titus had locked the room and marched outside Lucius had already mounted his horse and the gates were opening. Using the stirrup Titus leapt onto his horse. Lucius led the convoy setting a fast pace that the soldiers riding on the carts struggled to keep up with. Titus made his horse gallop, weaving in and out of the carts to reach Lucius.

'Lucius, I have told you these paths are treacherous especially with a horse and cart, you need to slow down,' Titus shouted.

'Me and my soldiers are experienced horse men, we can handle this type of terrain,' Lucius shouted back.

Before long they reached the olive groves slowing down the pace as they approached Zygos' house through the trees. Zygos raised his arm to acknowledge their arrival and walked over to the outhouse and opened the gate.

'Welcome again,' Zygos greeted them with a huge smile, knowing he was in line for a large payday.

Lucius dismounted, approached Zygos and shook his hand.

'I could only bring five carts; do you think we can fit one hundred vases into the carts? I will still pay you four hundred aureus if you cannot,' Lucius said.

'Let us find out, but you must first taste my produce,' Zygos said leading Lucius into the outhouse.

Lucius' senses were confronted by the smell of freshly baked bread. Zygos removed a cloth covering one of the vases and using a ladle scooped out some olive oil and poured it into a bowl on the table.

'Come,' Zygos beckoned Lucius over.

Lucius rushed over in a manner to show Zygos that he did not really have the time for this. He broke off a portion of the bread and dipped it into the olive oil and ate it. Zygos looked at him with great anticipation. Lucius nodded his head to confirm his satisfaction.

Lucius said pleasantly surprised by the quality of the oil.

'I have a question Zygos. How many vases did Titus buy for the camp six months ago?' Lucius asked.

'I can not remember,' Zygos said looking around Lucius to see where Titus was.

'Be honest Zygos, you are good with numbers and I know you have a good memory.'

'Titus bought one hundred vases and paid me four hundred aureus for them,' Zygos reluctantly informed Lucius.

Lucius marched out of building.

'Men load the vases onto the carts,' he shouted out.

Titus was talking to one of the soldiers.

'Titus follow me,' Lucius said.

Lucius led him into the outbuilding and lifted one of the vases.

'Titus help the men. More hands less time,' Lucius said loudly.

The soldiers began to race each other while holding the vases, one nearly came a cropper as he tripped over his own feet but managed to keep his balance. Even Lucius was marching in a fast-rhythmical pace. In less than thirty minutes ninety vases had been carried onto the five carts.

'Bring the money,' Lucius ordered and two of the soldiers took out a chest.

'Zygos, here is your payment,' Lucius said as the Soldier placed the chest in front of Zygos.

Zygos was slightly hesitant as he looked at the chest.

'Go on open it,' urged Lucius.

Zygos opened it and the reflection of sun on the gold coins almost blinded him.

'I bid you farewell Zygos, keep growing the olives,' Lucius said as he raised his hand.

If the journey there had been precarious the road back to the camp was even more hazardous as now the heavy carts made the horses struggle to pull and more difficult to steer on the narrow road for the soldiers. Lucius and Titus rode side by side.

'Are you going to make Salamis before nightfall?' Titus asked.

'No, I plan to make it to Tamassos tonight and leave for Salamis at dawn tomorrow,' Lucius replied.

'These carts are going to slow you down.'

'I just hope the men are back from Arsinoe or we will be delayed further,' commented Lucius.

As the camp gates opened Lucius drew a big sigh of relief seeing the horses and cart in the courtyard. Dismounting Lucius approached the men on the carts.

'Quickly get some food and drink now and bring some for the journey. We are leaving very soon,' Lucius ordered.

Titus tied up his horse and started to walk to his quarters when the top of his hand was grabbed by Lucius.

'Titus take me to the basement store where the camps money is held.'

Lucius and Titus were followed in close proximity by two of Lucius' soldiers.

'What is wrong, Lucius?'

Lucius walked next to him still holding his hand as they walked down the stone stairs and into the corridor that housed the camp records room and then they approached the iron gate of the room that held all the camps money.

'Unlock the gate,' ordered Lucius.

Titus fumbled around in his pocket before producing the set of keys, but it took him a while before he could find the correct key for the door. The room was dark, and Lucius and Titus waited as one of the soldiers fetched a lantern.

'I do not understand what this is about,' said a concerned Titus.

Lucius stood silent until the soldier returned with a lantern. The room lit up to expose numerous chests.

'The camp records show that you purchased six hundred vases of olive oil from Zygos and paid him three thousand aureus. I spoke to Zygos and you actually purchased one hundred vases and paid him four hundred aureus. So, where is the balance of two thousand six hundred? Is it here or have you stored it in your quarters? Be honest with me Titus.'

Titus was lost for words overcome firstly by the embarrassment of being found out and secondly by the consequences and fate that awaited him.

'There is no denial Lucius. In two years I will return home, the money would guarantee a future for me and more importantly my family. I implore you as a follow Roman to understand my priorities and reason I took this course of action. Please will my apologies be good enough.' Titus said bowing his head.

Lucius pondered for a moment.

'I know the importance of family Titus and believe me they are my priority too, but you have not only dishonored yourself you have dishonored the empire and by the letter of the law you have committed a treasonous act and you should be put on trail for this act. As Governor I uphold the justice of this land, but I have a compassionate streak that runs through my body. My conclusion therefore is I will not report my findings of the camp records,' Lucius stated.

'Thank you,' Titus said taking the hand of Lucius and kissing it.

'But as I said my family is my priority, so I have one condition to keep my silence. I require two thousand aureus of the money you took,' Lucius said.

The look of relief on Titus' face turned sour.

'I will be content to give you half but not as much as two thousand,' Titus barked back.

'Titus you are not in a position to dictate terms with me. There are just two options. You either give me two thousand aureus or you retire in disgrace and I send you to stand trial,' Lucius calmly explained.

Titus knew there was only one inevitable outcome and under such circumstances he took the lantern and slowly walked to the back of the room and this revealed another iron door which he opened. Lucius followed him into the room. Numerous chests were stacked up against the wall. Lucius counted fifteen chests.

'Each chest contains five hundred gold aureaus. Take four chests,' Titus said with an air of despondency.'I applaud you for your collection of booty and providing for yourself and your family in retirement,' Lucius said with a touch of sarcasm.

With that comment Lucius strode out of the room.

'Load up four chests onto the front cart and prepare to leave the camp,' he instructed the two soldiers waiting outside.

Titus stood in the middle of the courtyard and looked on haplessly as the soldiers loaded the four chests onto the cart. The soldiers climbed onto the six carts, two soldiers per cart with three on horseback as they waited. Lucius held the reins of his horse and mounted. The horse nonchalantly walked over and stopped in front of Titus.

'I bid you farewell Titus. Who knows our paths may cross again in the future in some part of the empire? I thank you for the hospitality you and your men have provided.' Lucius said.

Titus found it difficult to muster any form of words and just raised his arm in acknowledgement to which Lucius raised his arm. The gates opened and Lucius led the convoy out of the camp. Titus followed behind and as he reached the gate.

'Hail Lucius,' he yelled out at the top of his voice.

Lucius looked back as the sound echoed across the land.

The narrow path climbed a long incline towards the mountains. Lucius grew a concerned look on his face as the convoy of carts in single file began to slow down behind him as the chests of coins in the first cart and the vases of oil in the others weighed down the wheels. Sounds of panting horses ever increased as did the pictures of apprehension on the faces of the soldiers. Reaching Tamassos by nightfall was now an impossibility but Lucius was determined to drive forward as far as possible, and this was demonstrated by the quicken of pace of his horse, this only meant that the carts fell further and further behind. Lucius rode back to the convoy.

'Men, you need to go faster, make the horses work,' Lucius yelled.

The soldier on the lead cart grew exasperated.

'Lucius can you not see the horses are struggling, if we push them any further, they will collapse,' the soldier yelled back.

'Push them,' Lucius shouted.

The Soldier whipped the horses with the reins, and this galvanized them into action as they surged along the path. Lucius' horse broke into a canter leaving the others behind, but soon he came to a sharp turning on the path. Lucius pulled the reins to halt his horse and stared down and directly below the sheer drop was a beautifully clear stream the very one that flowed through the olive trees of the village. Clear to such an extent he could see the stream bed. An almighty noise was heard and as Lucius looked back he was confronted by the front horses and cart hurtling towards him and rode his horse out of the way as the soldier riding on the cart and his colleague tried to stop but the horses and cart turned the corner and the two back wheels went over the edge thus dragging back the cart and two horses. Lucius and the three other soldiers on horseback dismounted and attempted to pull the horses forward from the edge of the cliff but the horses became spooked by the situation and started moving backwards, the two soldiers on the cart jumped off and at this point Lucius ran behind the cart and tried to lift the wheels back onto the path but as the soldiers tried to control the horses one bolted and as the soldiers let go the horses and the cart moved backwards and the chests of gold coins slid down the cart. Lucius held on to the back of the cart, but the momentum carried him the cart and the horses over the edge and down the steep hill.

Surveying the scene from upon the hill, the soldiers could see the mangled remains of the cart and horses and the gleaming specs of the coins scattered down the hill.

'Can you see him?' One of the soldiers uttered.

No one could see Lucius.

'I will ride back to the camp to inform them,' one of Lucius' Lieutenants said and with haste he mounted his horse and rode back to the camp.

Silence descended on the land apart from the stridulating sound of crickets and the flow of water down the stream. Four of the soldiers climbed down the hill to search for Lucius, the fertile earth giving way under their feet as they negotiated their way down. The body of one of the horses lay still and a cloud of flies had arrived sensing death. One of the soldiers was picking up coins whenever he found them and put them in his pouch. A wheel lay embedded in some nettles. The body of the second horse lay by the bank of the stream.

'Over here,' shouted one the soldiers.

Under the cart were seen the legs of Lucius. All four soldiers lifted and rolled over the cart to reveal his body. A soldier knelt to check for a pulse.

'The gods have taken him,' he pronounced.

A while later the sound of horses disturbed the air. The soldiers, who were sat down in silence by the edge of the stream next to Lucius' body, were almost startled to see Titus accompanied by a group of soldiers riding through the stream towards them. Titus dismounted and walked over to the body and went down on one knee and bowed his head. He took a deep breath as he stood up.

'Such tragedy. He must be given a funeral to befit a man of such rank and honour,' Titus said aloud.

His train of thought was interrupted when he saw a chest of coins which somehow had stayed intact. Bounding over he undid the latch and the coins were all there. 'Men let us clear the area. We will take Lucius back to the camp. Turn the carts round and take them back and can we see if we can find as many of the coins as we can,' instructed Titus.

He took out a large cloth and a length of rope from his saddle.

'You two,' he said pointing in the direction of two soldiers observing the scene.

'Cover the body and tie it up and lift it into one the carts on the path so we can take him back to the camp,' he ordered throwing them the cloth and rope.

Lucius' Lieutenant stood beside Titus.

'Where will we hold the funeral?' he asked Titus.

'His garrison was at Salamis so we must take him there for burial. As the senior officer I will accompany you and your men to Salamis. It will be to dangerous to carry the olive oil back to Salamis so that can stay at the camp,' Titus explained.

Both men bowed their heads as the body was carried away.

'Another two months and he would have left the Island,' said the Lieutenant.

Titus nodded and put his hands on his chest.

'All men are equal only twice in their lives when they are born and when they die, in between our lives are governed by the fate of the gods and maybe this was the fate for Lucius,' Titus pontificated. 'He was a good soldier and a good man and most importantly he was loyal to all his men,' the Soldier retorted.

'I have no doubt Lucius was a man of the empire. In fact, I know so, the emperor himself had future plans for him. If fate had not been so cruel, I could image Lucius one day becoming a Senator in Rome. Lessor able men have reached that pinnacle, but the secret is making yourself known and then establishing a form of relationship with the emperor. Gain his trust and you have a key to his inner circle,' said Titus.

'Maybe you are right Titus, but I believe however much the gods conspire, you make your own fate and your own luck in this World,' the soldier countered.

'I agree, I agree with your beliefs.'

One of the other soldiers came up to them.

'Titus, we have recovered three of the chests of coins, only one was broken and the coins are scatted all on the hill.'

'Do not concern yourselves with them, they can be left to honour the life of Lucius. Take the other boxes back to the camp,' Titus said with a smile and as he began to walk back to his horse he turned around.

'Talking of fate, the one place within the empire I have always wanted to go is Britannia.'

THREE

Terra, 688 AD

Husayn found the exact spot he had been searching for all day, a clearing in between two newly built houses overlooking the olive groves at the lower end of the village. For an autumns day the sun was still scorching and Husayn found a shaded area under a tree to plant himself and his bag of tools. The olive groves were a hive of activity due to the start of the harvest. Husayn was fascinated by the whole process as it seemed most of the villagers were involved in the picking of the olives. It was quite evident to him even from this distance who the landowner was, the man on a horse shouting out instructions to all and sundry. Husayn turned his attention to the job that brought him to Terra. He opened his bag and took out his tools that consisted of paper and a couple of quill pens and a small jar of ink and lay them on the ground before walking over to the clearing. He used his feet to measure out the area and chalk to mark it out. Husayn was an architect and was the chief designer of mosques in Cyprus serving under the Umayyad Caliphate, born and educated in Damascus he had the best job in the World, travelling the vast Arab empire designing and building mosques.

The afternoon was spent sketching the design of the new mosque, by his normal standards this would be a small building, but he had chosen the site so the entire village could view it even the Greek inhabitants in the southern part of the village. The peace was broken by the arrival of an Arab soldier.

'As-salam Alaikum,' the soldier greeted Husayn as he dismounted.

'Wa-Alaikum-as-Salaam,' Husayn responded.

'My name is Bakir Ali and you must be the architect. I was told to expect you. The villagers are excited by the thought of a mosque being built. Well, some of the villagers are excited, the ones that live in lower part of village not so,' Bakir Ali explained.

'Do you mean those villagers?' Husayn asked pointing below to the people harvesting the olives.

'Yes, they are Christians so not surprisingly they are hostile to the idea of a mosque,' Bekir Ali said.

'I assume there is a church in the village?' Husayn asked.

'Yes, follow this road and you will come across it.'

'Since the Byzantine Emperor and the Caliph signed the treaty making Cyprus a condominium the Byzantines have paid for the building of churches throughout the Island from the taxes. So, the Caliph is doing the same. In Tamassos the church and the mosque are opposite each other. This is fueling animosity between Christian and Muslim,' said Husayn.

'We have a garrison up where the old Roman fort was. If it was not for the army presence it would be dangerous for Arabs to live here. Numerous Arabs have moved here due to the fertile land in this area. It is possible for Arabs to buy land,' Bekir Ali commented.

'If I had enough money, I would buy the land where the olive trees grow. I have so enjoyed travelling the Caliphate, but I am growing old and tired. Time maybe to find some land to cultivate,' Husayn said looking down at the olive trees.

'Are you not tempted to return to the land of your father?'

'I have no family in Damascus any longer and I have never married, so you can call me a nomad,' answered Husayn.

'Kismet, maybe you will find a nice Muslim girl here,' Bekir Ali suggested.

Husayn laughed at such a prospect, but Bekir Ali had a wry smile on his face.

'Enough of this frivolity, I need a good builder and some good men to build the mosque. Is there any one you can recommend?' Husayn asked.

'This could be a dilemma for you. The best builder is Stanious but he is Greek,' Bekir Ali informed him.

'Why is it a dilemma?'

'You want to ask Christians to build a mosque?'

'Each man will be paid well, more to build the mosque than they will earn for the rest of year. Are you telling me they will refuse?' said Husayn.

Bekir Ali raised his hands and shrugged his shoulders.

Wandering eyes followed Husayn as he walked through the village followed by the soft sound of people mumbling under their breaths. His traditional Arab attire of long loose robe, baggy trousers and head cloth made him stand out in the part of the village that was inhabited by Christians. He approached a group of men standing outside the church.

'I would like to speak to Stanious,' he asked.

One of the advantages Husayn had from traveling the Arab empire was his proficiency in speaking Greek and this surprised the men. One of them pointed at a man standing and looking at the church.

'Stanious,' shouted one of the men. 'Someone wants to speak to you.'

The men parted as Stanious walked towards Husayn.

'How can I help you?' Stanious asked coldly.

Husayn smiled at him.

'Did you build this church?' he asked Stanious.

'Yes, me and these men standing here,' he replied.

'I am an architect and I have seen many churches in many countries, but I will be honest with you this is one of the best,' Husayn said.

'I am proud of it. Every time I walk by, I stop and look at it,' Stanious said.

'How would you like to earn two gold dinars a day to work for me. I will pay all your men one dinar a day,' Husayn proposed.

Stanious was taken aback by the proposition.

'What do you want me to build?' he asked Husayn.

'A Mosque.'

'You want me to build a mosque? Two dinars a day?' Stanious said with surprise.

'Yes, you will receive two dinars for every day you work. The mosque will be built in the upper village overlooking the olive groves. If you agree I will show you the plan that I have in my bag,' Husayn confirmed.

'I will need to speak to my men.'

'Go ahead and speak to them, I will be by the church,' Husayn said as he strolled over to the church, whilst Stanious spoke to his men. Husayn looked at the church impressed by the craftmanship at which point a priest walked out, all decked out in black with a long beard. Husayn gave him a smile and in return the priest gave him a scowl, this prompted Husayn to turn back towards Stanious and his men.

'When do you want us to start?' asked Stanious.

'The materials arrive in two days but can you and your men can start digging the foundations tomorrow?' asked Husayn.

Stanious nodded.

Over the next few days Stanious and his men laid the foundations of the mosque. Husayn set up a table and chair underneath the tree opposite to supervise the build. He would arrive at the crack of dawn and ensuring the builders had the requisite food and drink to sustain them during the long days. During this time, he built a rapport with Stanious and indeed with the other builders. He had moved into a modest house on the outskirts of the village near the Muslim quarter, but also spent time at the Arab army garrison outside the village. Husayn arrived at the site to witness the Arab soldiers helping to unload the large pieces of stone that would be used to build the mosque. One man could carry only one stone, so it was tiring back breaking work, but the assistance of the twenty or so Arab soldiers made a difference and cut the time taken to unload the stones. Husayn thanked the soldiers as they rode off and it was just then that a man approached Stanious and started remonstrating with him. Husayn kept his distance and walked back to under the tree pretending not to hear the raised voices, but he could overhear fragments of the conversation the man was unhappy that a mosque was being built in the village. The man came storming over to Husayn.

'Can I help you?' said Husayn standing up from his chair.

'What gives you the right to build a mosque overlooking my land?' the man said in a loud raspy voice, gesticulating in the direction of the olive trees.

'Is that your land?' Husayn said pointing in the same direction.

'Yes, I am Damaris and I do not want to look up every day and see this monstrosity you are building.'

'Sir, please do not offend me, this monstrosity as you call it will become a place of worship, it will be my place of worship. There is a beautiful church in the village for all Christians to worship and it is only right for all the Muslims in the village to have their own place of worship,' Husayn shouted back, purposely tightening his robe to show an outline of a dagger beneath his robe.

Damaris was taken aback by Husayn's aggressive retort.

'We do not want Muslims in our village,' said Damaris in a quieter tone.

'Let me explain the situation, firstly this is not your village. A treaty was signed by Emperor Justinian and Caliph Abd al-Malik allowing Cyprus to become a neutral territory. This means by the law of the treaty Arab and Byzantine must live in peace together and it also means Muslim and Christian have the right to practice their religion. I have been ordered by the Caliphate to build a mosque in this village and I have every intention of staying here until it is built and has opened for prayer. That is all I have to say to you.'

Damaris shook his head to demonstrate his view on Husayn's irksome statement. Damaris left in the same manner as he arrived storming off. Husayn turned to pour himself some water but was distracted by a commotion coming from near the building site. Builders started running and there was shouting. He quickly walked towards the melee to find the builders surrounding Damaris, who lay motionless on his back.

'What happened?' asked Husayn.

'I saw him collapse,' answered one of the builders.

Stanious attended to him.

'He's not breathing,' he shouted.

'Let me look at him,' Husayn said pushing himself through the men.

Husayn put his ear close to Damaris' lips and interlocked both his hands together to make a ball he then hit Damaris in the middle of his chest with a violent thud jerking Damaris' body upwards. After a moment Husayn repeated the hit this time with more force. Damaris let out an audible breath.

'Get him some water,' asked Husayn.

They poured water over his face which helped revive him.

'We need to get him to his home,' Husayn said.

The builders lifted Damaris onto the table and six of them carried him down the road with Husayn following behind.

As the men approached the house Damaris' wife came running out.

'What has happened?' she shouted out.

'He collapsed and stopped breathing, but Husayn saved him,' one of the men said.

'Which one is Husayn?' she asked.

'I am Husayn,' he said walking towards her.

'Can you warm up some olive oil and hot water,' he said to Damaris' wife. 'Put him into bed,' he asked the men.

Husayn cut Damaris' shirt, while Damaris' wife brought a bowl of warm olive oil and rubbed it over his chest. Damaris opened his eyes and closed them again.

'He needs to sleep and rest, but I think he will recover,' Husayn told Damaris' wife as he stood up.

'Thank you. If you had not been there, he would have died. My name is Callisto and I thank you.'

'We had an argument about the building of the mosque, maybe this brought on his illness, so I regret arguing with your husband and beg your forgiveness and I hope he fully recovers,' Husayn said bowing his head.

Callisto walked up to him and held his hand.

'No, you can not blame yourself, he has been ill for quite some time and his illness could happen any day so I will not blame you.'

He raised his head and it was only at this point he noticed her emerald green eyes which beautifully contrasted her jet-black hair.

'Thank you, I'd best be on my way,' Husayn said.

Ambulating up the road two of the builders were walking past Husayn when one of them run up and shook his hand. Further up the road he came across a couple of teenage boys who bowed their heads as he walked past, and an old man patted him on the shoulder. Husayn was baffled by this reaction, usually in the Christian part of the village people ignored him or mumbled some words in Greek. Stanious and other builders stood by the building site and as they saw Husayn approaching they stood in a line and one by one they thanked him some patting him on his back.

'I would like to invite you to my house tonight for dinner,' Stanious asked him.

Husayn could not believe the whole situation and the dinner invite.

'Yes, I would love to come.'

'Whenever you are ready you are welcome, do you know my house?'

'Yes, I know where you live,' Husayn confirmed.

The dilemma for Husayn was which robe to wear. Apart from his black robe he only had two others to choose from, a blue or red robe, but it was still a dilemma. Both robes lay on the bed and he made the difficult decision and put on the blue robe. Husayn knocked on the door of Stanious' house with great trepidation. The door opened slowly and Stanious stood there with a beaming smile.

'Husayn my friend welcome, come in,' said Stanious beckoning him in. Fumes of alcohol immediately confronted Husayn as Stanious pulled him into the house by the sleeves of his robe, through the house they passed like a gale force wind and into the back to be greeted by a large crowd of people.

'Husayn, this is my wife, get him a drink. Look, I know that you do not drink wine, so I have made you grape juice,' Stanious said as his wife brought over a large goblet of juice.

'Please try it, the grapes are from my vineyard,' insisted Stanious.

Husayn tentatively took a sip as Stanious waited with bated breath.

'It is delicious,' proclaimed Husayn.

This made Stanious even more overjoyed.

'I have a large vase of it in my cellar and I will arrange to bring it to you,' he said.

'There is no need to trouble yourself, it is nice, but I prefer to drink water,' Husayn explained.

'No, you will have it tomorrow,' insisted Stanious.

'Please sit down,' said Stanious' wife pointing to a chair by the table.

Jugs of wine flowed freely as the guests came and introduced themselves to Husayn. He recognized many of the faces, but this was the first instance that many of them had spoken to him, indeed, it was the first time that many would have even smiled or acknowledged him. Smoke with the accompanying smell drifted towards the table.

'What is on the fire?' Husayn enquired.

'For you, my friend we slaughtered a lamb, and I will promise you that it will be the tastiest meat you have ever eaten,' Stanious said proudly.

Carved slices of lamb were soon put on a plate in front of Husayn. As he ate a piece, he was overwhelmed by the how succulent the meat was, it was reminiscent of the family feasts he enjoyed back home in Damascus. He sat back and watched everyone tucking into the food and enjoying themselves and the most overriding aspect was how happy everyone seemed to be. He had never imagined that the day would come when he would be alone with a group of Christians and would feel happy, content, and comfortable in their company. Today was that day. Husayn made an effort to talk to everyone there, for him this was not just a personal odyssey but an opportunity to build bridges between the two communities, as once the mosque had been built, he would be departing the village. Stanious went to answer the loud knock on his door. Stanious came back outside but his mood had changed.

'It is Doctor Arthemois.'

Dr Arthemois walked out looking biblical with long flowing hair with grey streaks in it and even greyer beard.

'I have sad news. Our friend Damaris has died. He collapsed at home and his wife ran to my house but by the time we arrived back we had lost him. I need some volunteers to help carry the coffin from the church to Damaris' house so the priest can prepare the body before the funeral,' the doctor asked.

'I would like to help,' said Husayn standing up.

The doctor stared at him not sure what to say. Stanious grabbed Husayn by the robe.

'Husayn is coming so I need four more men,' Stanious said.

Reluctantly four hands went up and the Doctor and six men soon departed.

Light from several lanterns illuminated the façade of the church. The priest, Father Portamalis, stood by the entrance, clad in a black robe and black kalimavkion, a hat like a stovepipe hat but without the brim. As the men approached the church the priest was shocked to see that

Husayn was one the men. Dr Arthemois bowed in front of the priest.

'What is he doing here?' Father Portamalis whispered to the Doctor.

'He volunteered to help,' the Doctor responded.

'Muslims are not welcome in the house of Christ,' Father Portamalis uttered firmly.

The Doctor looked at him and turned around to the men.

'Stainious, your friend can not enter the church,' Dr Arthemois said loudly so the people who had began to gather around the church could hear him.

'I understand, best if I go,' Husayn said.

'Stop!' Stanious said grabbing Husayn's arm.

'This man is part of our village and I will not allow prejudice to play a part in his time here. He is a free man, and he has as much right as anyone to walk or enter any building in the village. Father if you do not allow him to enter the church, I will not enter nor will my family,' Stanious said passionately.

Dead silence fell.

'I agree with Stanious,' shouted one of the other men.

'Me too,' said another.

'And I,' said yet another.

Father Portamalis was shocked by this level of support for Husayn, who was even more shocked than the Father by the response.

'Father, a man has died, one of the most respected men in the village and every single one of these men standing behind me are here to pay their respects the best way they can and carrying the coffin is one sign of this,' pleaded Dr Arthemois.

Father Portamalis stepped aside and the Doctor, Stanious, Husayn and the other men walked past him into the church. Husayn was immediately drawn to the depiction of Christ carrying the cross on the painting on the wall at the back of the alter, the vivid colours of the paining had Husayn's eyes transfixed. The coffin lay on a table surrounded by four lit torches. Stanious and Husayn with the help of two others lifted the coffin. Two other men took a torch each and led the way followed by Father Portamalis and the Doctor and then the four men carrying the coffin on their shoulders and the procession exited the church. The men followed the footpath through the olive trees towards Damaris' house. They walked in a somber silence as the house came into view. Standing outside the house was Callisto and her three teenage children. She was dressed all in black with a shawl covering her head. Father Portamalis gave a blessing as Callisto led the men into the house and to the bedroom. Damaris' body lay on the bed. Father Portamalis continued with his blessings. The men moved a table into the bedroom and placed the coffin on the table. Husayn, Stanouis, Dr Arthemois and one other lifted Damaris and placed him into the coffin. Husayn bowed and left the room to find Callisto standing outside.

'I am most sorry for your loss,' Husayn said in a quiet voice.

Callisto looked up and smiled at him.

'Thank you for helping my husband earlier, but God has taken him now, it was meant to be,' she said tearfully.

'His time came far too early, at times Allah works in mysterious ways, ways humankind cannot explain.'

'Your Allah and our God are one. Every life has a purpose and once that purpose has been served it is time to leave the World to serve your maker,' expressed Callisto.

'God will ensure that he will rest in peace,' Husayn uttered.

Callisto held his hand.

'I would like you to come to Damaris' funeral.'

'Father Athemois may not approve, he was quite upset when I entered the Church to help carry the coffin.'

'You will be my guest, so the good Father will not have a say in the matter of who I invite or do not invite, but sorry, maybe I am being too presumptuous, would you like to come to the funeral?' she asked him.

'If you are inviting me, I will attend.'

'Thank you,' she said letting go of his hand.

Timber beams were stacked up by the near completed exterior walls of the mosque by the Arab soldiers. Husayn counted the beams and counter checked it against the plan to ensure the requisite number had been delivered and that these were adequate to commence the construction of the mosque roof. Stanious turned up and waved at Husayn whilst still consuming his breakfast. Husayn beckoned him over.

'Good morning, do you think you and your men would be able to complete the walls today?' Husayn asked.

'I am certain we will have them finished by the end of the day,' Stanious said while swallowing the last piece of his breakfast.

Husayn smiled and walked to his table under the tree, content that the work was ahead of schedule, but the smile did not last too long with the sight of Father Portamalis walking towards him.

'Good day Father, you do not normally come to this part of the village,' Husayn said.

'I hear that you will be attending the funeral of Damaris,' the priest sternly said.

'His widow has invited me to attend and I have accepted her invitation. Do you have an objection to that Father?'

'A matter of fact I do. It is blasphemy for a Muslim to enter the house of Christ. Under pressure I allowed you in the other night, but you will not be welcome again. If you do, you will unleash the wrath of God and you will not find that experience pleasant,' he warned Husayn.

'Maybe Father it is best if you speak to Callisto. She has invited me to her husband's funeral, and it would be most discourteous of me to not accept the invitation. I arrived in this village to do my job and as you can see this is coming to fruition and when completed I will be leaving the village but until then I will be part of this community,' Husayn calmly said.

'You are part of the community in this village, but only the Muslim community. This island historically since the days of Alexander of Macedon has been Christian and Greek. We did not invite the Arabs to the island, you invaded and now due to this treaty making Cyprus a condominium, we are tied together. I do not care and do not want to dictate how you live your life, as long as there is no interference in my way of life or any other Christian's way of life. Attending the funeral at my Church is interfering and I will do everything in my power to stop you. Husayn, let me tell you another thing, building the mosque here is fine, but one day when all the Muslims have gone this building will also go,' said the agitated Father.

'You are very good with words Father. In Arabic we have one word that means all those words put together, kismet. It means your destiny is already written and your fate is sealed. Can I ask one question Father?'

'Yes.'

'Are you as a Christian a better man then me, a Muslim?'

Father Portamalis stared at him for a few seconds turned and walked away.

A loud knock of the door woke Husayn from his dream. Wondering who would want to visit him in the middle of the night he lit a candle and reached for his dagger and hid it behind his back. He nervously opened the door and standing there was Callisto holding something wrapped in a cloth.

'Come in.'

'Why are you here at this time,' he asked.

'I baked olive bread and I thought that you might like to try some,' she said unwrapping the bread and placing it on the table.

Husayn used his dagger to cut the warm bread into segments before biting into a piece.

'This is wonderful,' he said.

'Eat all it, I baked it for you,' a smiling Callisto said.

'I had a conversation with Father Portamalis today,' Husayn started to say.

'I know I had a visit from him this evening,' interrupted Callisto.

'He, I would not say threatened, but insisted that I should not attend your husband's funeral. I must say sorry, but I did say he should speak to you.'

'The Father spoke to me on similar lines, but I told him I could and would invite who I wish to the funeral and he left with a huff and puff.'

'I wish I had witnessed that. Callisto, If the whole village is going to turn against you, I would rather not come. Tension and animosity between Christians and Muslims are normal but not within the same community,' said Husayn.

'No, I will not be dictated how to live my life by the Church,' she said adamantly.

'All I want is peace and harmony in my time here and I want to avoid any form of conflict,' he said.

'I agree with my whole heart, but there are times when you have to stand and fight and this is that time. For me and for no one else I would like you to come to the funeral.'

'Callisto, you are good woman, for a Christian that is,' he said smiling bringing a smile to her face. 'You are strong, and I will come to the funeral on one condition.'

'What is that?'

'You bake me more olive bread.'

'I will bake a hundred loafs for you,' she responded with a giggle. 'But I have one more request of you. I would like you to be one of the men who carry Damaris' coffin from my house to the church,' asked Callisto.

Husayn stared at her and slowly nodded his head to agree to her request.

'Yes, I would like to do that,' he confirmed.

'Now I must go home.'

'Thank you for coming. You have cleared my cloudy mind,' he said opening the door for her.

'Good night,' she said as she kissed him on his cheek before leaving. The kiss rendered him motionless, but he managed to make his way back to the table to continue eating the olive bread before he was interrupted by another knock at the door. He quickly rushed to the door with an enormous grin and opened the door.

'Did you forget something?'

It was not Callisto. Three men wearing black hoods rushed him and pushed him back inside, they reigned in punches and forced him to the ground. Thinking quickly, he picked up a chair by its leg, got to his feet before smashing it into the head of one the assailants. Another attacker grabbed Husayn by the throat with both hands and began to strangle him but Husayn held the attacker's wrists and with all his strength he managed to pull his hands away from his throat. He noticed that the attacker had a large cross and two smaller crosses tattooed on the palm of his right hand. Husayn punched the attacker in the stomach flooring him before reaching out to grab his dagger and brandishing it in front of the assailants. Two of the attackers got to their feet and realizing that Husayn seemed like an expert with a dagger all three fled through the front door.

His right eye was bruised, black with a tint blue and yellow so Husayn soaked a cloth into water before applying it onto it.

'Do you want me to help you with that?' asked Bekir Ali, who had just arrived at Husayn's house after hearing the news of the attack.

'It will heal, it is just superficial, no damage to my eye,' replied a calm Husayn.

'Why did the widow visit you?' Bekir Ali asked inquisitively.

'She baked olive bread and brought me some.'

'Maybe she brought more than the bread, like three men,' said Bekir Ali his mind working overtime.

'I don't think she had anything to do with it. She wants me to attend her husband's funeral.'

'At the church?' said a surprised Bekir Ali.

'Yes.'

'Are you going to go?'

'Callisto wants me to be there so I will. No one will stop me.'

'In that case my men will be there to quell any trouble that may arise. That priest, what is his name?'

'Father Portamalis,' answered Husayn.

'Yes, Father Portamalis must have had something to do with the attack. He has made veiled threats to Muslims before and I have warned him before. I can have another quiet word in his ear or if you wish I can make him disappear,' said a determined Bekir Ali.

'No retribution. I will handle everything my way.'

'You are a braver man than me. There will be a great number of eyes on you. There is no one you can trust, no one, not even the widow,' Bekir Ali warned Husayn.

'There are times when you have to put your trust in someone be it Muslim or Christian. Maybe in years to come, I mean years after we have departed this World all men regardless of race or religion can live in peace,' Husayn said.

'As long you have two men of different colour or different belief you will never achieve total peace in this World,' replied Bekir Ali.

'I am an optimist so I would like to believe that man will change in the future. Today will be a start when I go into the Church,' Husayn said.

'You are free to do whatever you feel is right, but I think you are making a great mistake,' Bekir Ali warned him.

'All people make mistakes in their lifetime, but how many of them learn from these mistakes. If today is a mistake I hope I can move forward. I know my task is to oversee the completion of the mosque, but I seem to have become part of the villager's lives,' Husayn said.

'Your mistake was saving Damaris' life that day. What was the point he only lived another few hours. Now you have brought all these problems onto yourself,' said Bekir Ali.

'What was I supposed to do, let the man die?'

'Yes.'

A crowd of people had begun to congregate outside the house of Callisto. Father Portamalis accompanied by two junior priests walked into the house to make the final preparations before leading the procession of the coffin to the church. Stanious and three other men waited by the front of the house and soon they were joined by Dr Athemois.

'Are we waiting for one more person?' asked the Doctor.

'Callisto has asked Husayn to help carry the coffin,' Stanious informed the Doctor.

'I know Father Portamalis will object to that,' the Doctor said.

'Have you not heard, Husayn was attacked by men last night. Probably to warn him not to come to the funeral. and enter the church,' Stanious explained.

'No, this is first I have heard of it. Maybe he has had a change of heart and decided not to come,' the Doctor said.

'I do not think so,' Stanious said pointing to the path.

Everyone looked to see Husayn marching towards the house. He wore a black robe with no head covering leaving his jet-black hair to see the light of day and he was clean shaven. This magnified the black eye and a couple of red marks on his neck. He nodded his head to acknowledge everyone and stood next to Stanious.

'Perfect timing,' whispered Stanious.

'Do you want me to look at your eye?' Dr Athemois asked Husayn.

'No Doctor, I will be fine it is just a little sore.'

Father Portamalis came out of the house.

'The body is ready.'

The six pallbearers followed the priest into the house, and he led them into the room. Damaris' body lay in the casket, he was dressed in a gold silk robe. Callisto went up to the casket and kissed her husband on the forehead before nodding to Father Portamalis who in turn signaled to the two junior priests to seal the coffin. They placed the top of the coffin before using a hammer to put some nails in to secure it.

'Men, when you are ready please lift the coffin onto your shoulders,' Father Potamalis instructed.

They all looked at each other to establish who would be in the front.

'I will go at the back,' insisted Husayn.

Stanious and Dr Arthemois went to the front followed by a couple of the builders and Husayn and another builder brought up the rear and all six lifted the coffin and placed it onto their shoulders. The priests began their blessings before Father Portamalis and the two junior priests led the pallbearers out, and behind them walked Callisto and her three children, and other relatives and friends from the village. The procession left the house and down the narrow path through the olive trees. Husayn looked up to see Bekir Ali and a group of his soldiers watching them from the path above near the mosque. Husayn sensed the eyes of the village converging down upon him, and mumblings of discontent ringing in his ears.

'Why is the Arab here?' asked one of the mourners, but in Husayn's mind he could see the question being asked on the lips of all the mourners and this seemed to amplify throughout the procession. The pallbearers entered the church and Father Portamalis led them down the aisle towards the alter before laying the coffin on the stone slab.

Calisto and her children stood at the front near the coffin. Husayn stood next to Callisto.

'I think it is best if I leave now but my thoughts will be with you,' uttered Husayn to her.

Callisto grasped his hand for a second and smiled at him whilst holding back her tears. Husayn quietly and without trying to attract attention walked to the side of the Church but caught the eye of Father Potamalis as he was leaving, the pair exchanging cold hard stares.

The mosque cast a shadow over the olive trees and at its center was the shape of the dome, the building looked resplendent in the sunshine and stepping out of its shadow Husayn saw a horse and cart approaching the mosque and he swiftly made his way up the path to meet it. The man on the cart lifted a box.

'Do you want me to open it?' the man asked Husayn.

'Yes, please,' Husayn said with great anticipation.

The man opened the box and Husayn lifted out its contents, a saif Arabic sword measuring three feet long and made of solid gold. This was the last piece of the build that would be placed on top of the dome. Stanious placed the ladder in preparation.

'My instinct tells me that you would want to place the sword on the dome,' Stanious said to Husayn with a grin.

'My friend your instincts are correct. This sword is a gift from Allah, and it will protect the mosque for however long this place of worship stands,' Husayn said lifting the sword above his head.

Stanious fetched a small copper stand and fixed it to the middle of the sword and tightened it with two screws.

'There is a hole at the very top of the dome and the stand will fit precisely into it, then these two bolts will secure it to the dome,' Stanious explained to Husayn placing the two bolts into the palm of his hand. Husayn climbed the ladder onto the roof of the mosque, there was a smaller ladder placed against the dome and carefully holding the sword in one hand and the edge of the ladder in the other he tentatively negotiated the steps to reach the top of the dome. He placed the stand attached to the sword into the hole and taking the two bolts he twisted them into the holes until it was fully secure. As he moved back to admire it, the sun caught the sword and the light momentarily blinded Husayn, and as he lifted his hands to shield his face he lost his balance on the ladder and he fell with a heavy thud onto the roof. Stanious rushed up the ladder and found Husayn laying there motionless.

'Someone go and get the Doctor,' he shouted at the top of his voice. A little stain of blood appeared by the side of Husayns head and Stainous held his hand firmly.

'Husayn, Husayn,' he called out, but there was no response.

A short while later Dr Arthemois arrived on the scene climbing the ladder onto the roof.

'Doctor, he is breathing but he is not moving, and he is bleeding from the head,' Stanious informed the Doctor.

The Doctor opened his bag and took out a small jar and unscrewed the top.

'Brace yourself,' he told Stanious.

An almighty stench escaped from the jar, the smell almost knocking Stanious off his feet as the Doctor placed the jar under Husayn's nose. A few seconds later Husayn began to cough and he opened his eyes.

'Husayn, can you move your hands?' Dr Athemois asked.

Husayn started moving his fingers.

'Can you move your feet?'

Husayn moved his feet and wriggled his toes before gingerly sitting up.

'You have a small cut on your head, let me treat it,' the Doctor said.

He poured a liquid from another jar onto a cloth before dabbing the cloth onto Husayn's cut. This made him flinch with pain.

'It will sting for a while, but it will stop any infections,' the Doctor assured Husayn. When the Doctor took his right hand away Husayn noticed that there were three crosses tattooed on the palm of his hand, identical to the tattoo one of the assailants had during his attack. Husayn looked into the Doctor's eyes. Suddenly Husayn's grogginess vanished.

'I think I'll be fine Doctor,' said Husayn, now one hundred percent certain that Dr Athemois was one of the men who attacked him.

'We need to get you home. The best remedy is sleep, a few hours rest you will be back to normal,' advised the Doctor.

The Doctor and Stanious helped Husayn to his feet before guiding him down the ladder to firm land.

A knock at the door woke Husayn from a delightful dream. He still felt slightly groggy, but he had the presence of mind to hide his dagger in his robe as he answered the door.

'Hello,' Callisto said. 'I heard about your fall.'

'Come in,' he said looking out for anyone else lurking outside.

'Luck seems to have deserted you at the moment,' Callisto said with a pinch of irony.

'It certainly has, but I am also very happy now. The mosque is complete, and my work here is done.'

Callisto placed a cloth covered parcel on the table.

'Is this what I think it is?' asked Husayn excitedly as he unraveled the twisted layers of cloth to reveal a large round loaf of olive bread.

'Savour every last piece as this may be last one I bake,' she said.

'Why?' he said puzzled.

'I have decided that I will sell the house and land and move to where my family live in Polis. This is my husband's village and without him I do not want to be here. My mother and sisters live in Polis and my children will get more support from having family around. Without

Damaris I cannot maintain and harvest the olives so it is best I sell to someone who can.'

Husayn cut two slices of the loaf and gave one to Callisto.

'How long will it take to sell the land?' he asked.

'I have a buyer already. Dr Arthmois is going to buy it, in fact he is coming tomorrow to give me the money,' she said.

'Is he going to have the time to harvest the olives?' asked Husayn curiously.

'He told me that he is purchasing a machine that will make pressing the olives far easier and quicker. The land on the other side of the stream also belonged to Damaris so the Doctor can plant more olive trees there. That would mean the potential to supply olive oil to the whole region including Polis. It will make him a very wealthy man,' Callisto explained.

'Potentially he could supply other regions of the island,' said an envious Husayn.

'When are you thinking of leaving?' he asked her.

'If the Doctor buys it tomorrow it will take me a week for me to go.'

'So, nothing or no one could persuade you to stay?' he asked.

'No, I have made up mind,' she confirmed.

Husayn found that the olive bread tasted better than last time Callisto baked one.

'I will have to follow you to Polis so I can get some more of this bread,' he remarked.

'What are your intentions now the mosque had been finished?' Callisto asked.

'Admittedly I have grown to like the village especially the people, so I have a dilemma. Do I continue to travel and build mosques for the caliphate or do I decided to retire?

This would give me so much time I cannot even fathom it.'

'The whole village likes you and for many you have become part of it like the other Muslims who live here,' she said.

'My concern would be the day Cyprus ceases becoming a condominium and Arabs and Byzantines are at war again what will happen to the Muslims here? What will happen to the Mosque?

'I do not know the answer to your questions, but I do know that having Muslims living in the village will make it a much better place. Unfortunately, I will not be around to experience this,' she said.

'Could I ask for one last wish?' said Husayn.

'You can.'

'Could you show me how to bake olive bread before you leave?

'I am sure I will have time to show you.'

'Thank you,' he said with a beaming smile.

The moon and stars lit up the night sky as Husayn walked Callisto home along the path through the olive groves to the front door of her house.

'Thank you for walking me home,' she said before planting a kiss on his cheek.

'I will see you before you leave,' confirmed Husayn.

Callisto went into her house and Husayn decide, to walk home via the mosque. The night was clear and silent and as he approached the mosque, he could sense something was not right. Voices were coming from the mosque and as he walked nearer, he could make out a couple of figures on the roof and someone holding a torch at the bottom of the ladder. Husayn crept up behind the man on the ground and as the man turned Husayn grabbed him pushing his head against the wall with such force that it knocked him unconscious. Husayn took off his hood but he did not recognize the man, but he noticed that he had three crosses tattooed on the palm of his hand. He climbed the ladder, and as he reached the roof, he could see one man holding a torch and the other man trying to remove the gold sword on top of the dome. Husayn stood on the roof until the man holding the torch noticed him. Husayn beckoned him over and the man rushed over waiving the torch and trying to thrust the flame into Husayn's face. As Husayn moved forward, the man swung at him with the torch and Husayn ducked out the way, grabbed the man by his robe and threw him off the roof, a thud indicating that he had reached the ground. The third man had successfully removed the gold sword and descended onto the roof from the dome.

'If you put the sword down, I will let you leave, if you do not you will not leave here alive,' said Husayn giving the man an ultimatum.

The man, like his other two colleagues, was dressed head to toe in black. The pair danced around each other, Husayn was at a disadvantage having no weapon while the man in black had the gold sword knowing that it was still a lethal and could cut a man in half.

'Take your hood off Doctor,' Husayn shouted.

There was no response from the man.

'I know it is you so take your hood off and fight like a Christian or are you a coward, afraid to fight a Muslim knowing you might lose,' Husayn baited him.

Finally, the man took off his hood. It was Dr Athemois.

'How did you know it was me?' asked the Doctor.

'The tattoo on the palm of your hand. What is it supposed to signify?'

'A Christian Brotherhood set up to fight and eradicate the Island of Arabs. When we drive all the Muslims out of the village, we will destroy the mosque,' the Doctor said with menace.

'Today is not that day, Doctor. Your Brotherhood will die tonight, it will die with you,' proclaimed Husayn.

Husayn stood by the edge of the roof. The Doctor came for him and as he swung the sword Husyan grabbed the Doctor's hands and the pair struggled trying to wrestle the sword away from each other. From a distance it seemed that they were dancing with each other face to face, cheek to cheek, but both summoned all their strength and with one last effort they flew off the roof whilst both still holding onto the sword.

The morning call of the roosters reverberated around the village. Bekir Ali stood motionless still trying to digest the carnage that lay at the bottom of the Mosque. Half a dozen Arab soldiers loaded the cart with three bodies wrapped in black cloth and tied up with ropes.

'Take them away,' ordered Bekir Ali as he mounted his horse and cantered off.

The cart and soldiers followed at a serene pace.

Callisto was stirring at a large bowl of flour and water and to this she added a bowl of black olives and a smaller bowl of chopped onions and she began to give a vigorous stir to mix all the various ingredients before a knock at the door interrupted her. She opened the door to find Husayn standing there, his right hand covered with a blood-soaked bandage.

'What has happened? you are hurt,' she said concerned.

'No, I had a slight fall, I will survive.'

He limped inside, Callisto carefully guiding him and helped him sit down.

'I have a proposal for you,' Husayn said as Callisto listened intently. 'I would like to buy the olive groves. I do not want the house, but I will pay you the same price Dr Athemois was offering.'

Callisto was taken aback by his proposal.

'But I have promised to sell it to the Doctor.'

'Unfortunately, the Doctor had an accident and he is dead.'

'No, when, how,' she blurted out.

'He is dead, that is the fact. I have thought about my future, so many ideas floating around my head and this idea came to me this morning. I want to buy only your land, so you and your children can still live here if you wish,' he said.

'Where would you live?' she asked.

'I will stay in the house I am in now. The sale of the land will secure you and your children, and I will give you enough olives to bake your delicious bread, you can sell it in the village and all the villages around. What do you think?' Husayn said excitedly.

Callisto was unsure how to react. She sat down and looked at Husayn, who tightened the bandage around his hand.

'Yes,' Callisto shouted out.

'Yes,' he repeated.

'Yes, I will sell you the land.'

Husayn smiled and nodded.

'When is that bread going to be ready?' he said.

Bekir Ali and his men came to a halt on top of the mountain.

'Here will do,' Bekir Ali said.

The soldiers lifted the three bodies from the cart and one by one hurled them down the side of the mountain.

FOUR

Terra, 1191

The distance between Terra and Paphos was just under twenty miles and Neilos covered this journey two times a week, every Monday and Thursday taking olives, grown on his father's land, by horse and cart and selling them in the market in Paphos. This lucrative trade had made his father, Elpidios, the wealthiest man in the village and Neilos knew that one day he would inherit his father's land, maybe sooner then normally expected as Elpidios had been ill for some time, indeed, well over a year in which time Neilos had taken over transporting and selling the olives and for a sixteen year old this had greatly hastened his maturity. Time was not a factor for Neilos as the biggest enjoyment he derived from the journeys to Paphos was leaving the village. It had opened his eyes to the outside world and made him realize that the village was no place for him, and he craved to leave, but the situation with his father had dampened his enthusiasm to leave. He would discuss his predicament with his companion on the journeys, Zeus the horse. Zeus was probably as old as Neilos and could barely see out of his left eye but had the stamina of a horse half his age and had an incredible memory, able to remember any route after completing just one journey. Neilos could fall asleep in the back of the cart safe in the knowledge that Zeus would take him back to the village.

Approaching the crossroads Neilos noticed something odd. Two men were standing in the middle of the road, next to them by the side he could make out two more men and a horse. As he got closer it became clear that the two men standing were soldiers wearing armour and the taller of the two had a coat of arms insignia over his breastplate. Neilos was startled by a corpse of a dead horse on the roadside and pulled the reigns to bring Zeus to a halt. Neilos jumped down from the cart.

'Can I help you gentlemen?' asked Neilos as his attention was drawn to the coat of arms on the tall soldier. The blazon of the coat of arms was of three gold lions with blue tongues and blue claws on red gules.

'Two of the men are hurt,' one of the soldiers said.

Neilos walked over to the two soldiers sitting down and both had bloody wounds to their arms.

'What happened?' asked Neilos.

'They were both on the horse and it collapsed,' said the soldier hesitantly.

'You are Greek, but these other men are not from the Island,' Neilos nervously said.

'You are correct young man. We are all soldiers fighting besides King Richard of England and King Philip of France in the Holy Land. I am Phocus and this is Robert from England and the men there Phillipe and Jehan from France. We arrived in Cyprus from Acre to rescue the Lady Berengaria who was taken prisoner by Isaac Komnenos. The Lady was released, and she is to marry King Richard in Lemesos on the Twelfth day of this month. Komnenos gave his word to the King that he would contribute to the crusade to the Holy Land, but a man of his word he is not and escaped with his men to the interior of the Island,' Phocus explained to Nelios who listened with intense fascination.

'Guy de Lusignan agreed to hunt and capture Komnenos and his troops. Phillipe and Jehan are part of the Lusignan army and we were headed to Nicosia but we came across soldiers loyal to Komnenos and while in pursuit we became detached from the main force and we were ambushed injuring our two comrades in arms over there and losing two horses,' Phocus said confirming their predicament.

'Do you intend to travel back to the Holy Land?' Neilos asked.

'Jerusalem is still held by Saladin's army and God will not let us rest until we capture the City back from the Muslim infidel. We may be from different lands and speak different languages, but we serve the same God and we have given our oath that we will not return to our homes until the holy city is back in the hands of Christendom,' Phocus said with passion.

Neilos attended to Phillipe and was shocked by the sight of the wound a deep cut exposing the bone just below the elbow. He fetched a water container from the cart and offered it to the injured man, who took two large gulps. Neilos then offered it to the other men. He tied Phillipe's arm with a large cloth and made a sling with another piece of cloth.

'My village is just up this road and we have a doctor who can hopefully treat him,' Neilos said.

'Are there horses in the village?' Phocus asked.

'Yes.'

Jehan and Robert climbed onto the back of the cart and helped Phillipe get on. Phocus mounted his horse and followed the cart. The three men at the back, with their armour and weapons, weighed down the cart which meant Zeus struggled to pull it. If he were five years younger, he could have pulled a cart with ten men on it, but at his age the arthritis was playing havoc on his old legs. Resolutely Zeus soldiered on and the cart trundled up the road to the village.

One of the farmers raised his hand in acknowledgement as the cart went past, but when he realised the other men with Neilos were strangers his hand slowly came down. As the cart reached the fork in the road, Neilos directed Zeus to the path leading to the upper village, this meant another uphill climb for Zeus. The cart stopped outside a large building.

'This is where we store all our olives. You can rest here,' Neilos told the men.

'Horses, where can we get horses?' Robert asked.

Neilos hesitated before answering.

'I will ask my father,' he said as he opened the door of the building.

Phocus tied his horse to the back of the cart and assisted the others as they helped Phillipe out of the cart. Phillipe's grimace was a sign of the immense pain his arm was giving him. Wooden vats of olives greeted the men as they entered the building. They looked up to the domed ceiling.

'What kind of building is this?' asked Phocus.

'Many people say this used to be a mosque.' Neilos replied.

'A mosque!' blurted out Phocus in shock.

'Are you saying Muslims lived on this island once?' asked Robert.

'Yes, Muslims lived in this village, but they left a few hundred years ago. No one knows exactly when. The mosque had been deserted for a few hundred years, but it was so well built it has survived. My father wanted somewhere to store the olives after the harvest and he came to an arrangement with the village elders that he would pay for repairs to the village church if he had sole use of the mosque,' Neilos explained to the men sensing that the men felt uneasy about being in the old mosque.

'If you wait here, I will fetch the Doctor and bring you some food and water.'

Sweat trickled down from Nelios' forehead as he questioned the wisdom of bringing the men to the village. He untied Phocus' horse from the cart and tied it to the gate of the old mosque. After checking the harness on Zeus, he jumped on the cart, without the weight of the men in the cart, Zeus shot off. Neilos headed towards the house of Doctor Demitrou. In his head the reoccurring question was how he was going to be able to obtain horses the men required for them to leave the village. Dr Demitrou just happened to be leaving his house when Neilos pulled up in his cart.

'Doctor, I need your help. There are some men with injuries who need assistance.'

'Can you tell the kind of injuries these men have?' asked the Doctor.

'Wounds inflicted by a sword,' confirmed Neilos.

'Let me get my equipment,' the Doctor said rushing inside.

Phocus was pacing up and down in the old mosque.

'Where is that boy? We need horses and we need to leave here and find our men,' said Robert opening one of the vats and helping himself to some of the olives. Phillipe's temporary sling was totally blood soaked and sweat was pouring off his face, to signify, not only how hot it was, but that he was losing too much blood. He tried to get to his feet and after taking two small steps he collapsed to the ground.

'Give him water,' Jalan said, himself nursing a wound on his right hand.

The door swung open and Neilos and Dr Demitrou hurried in. The Doctor immediately deduced that Phillipe needed attention. He sat him up and removed the sling to discover the seriousness of the wound. The Doctor shook his head. 'I need to close the wound before it becomes infected,' the Doctor said with a pessimistic tone in his voice.

'Doctor, will he be well enough to travel later?' Phocus asked.

'Do you mean later today?' The Doctor questioned.

Phocus nodded his head in confirmation.

'I would advise against him travelling anywhere. I can feel a fever developing and I just hope it is not a sign of infection,' explained the Doctor.

Jalan and Robert took Phocus aside and the three of them began talking. Neilos stood closer to the men watching the Doctor attending to Phillipe but trying to eavesdrop on the conversation. Phocus beckoned Neilos over.

'We would all like to thank you for helping us but we do need to join the rest of our men who are heading to Nicosia, so we need horses. We are willing to pay for them, but we need them today,' Phocus explained.

'I understand, I will go to my father who has horses.'

'Tell him that we will pay for them,' reiterated Phocus.

          Built by the stream with the olive trees in view, Elpidios stood proud by his new house surveying all the land that he owned. He gingerly walked towards the stables, holding a walking stick in his right hand to assist him with his balance. A stable hand was just taking a newly acquired horse for a walk.

'How is he?' Elpidios asked the stable hand.

'He is a frisky little thing,' the stable hand answered.

The response put a smile on Elpidios' face and the smile stayed on as he saw Neilos, Zeus and the cart coming up the path towards the house. Elpidios sat down in his favorite chair, strategically placed between the house the stables with a view of the land, the stream, and the mountains beyond. Neilos retrieved a bag of money from the back of cart and walked up to Neilos and placed the bag on his Father's lap. Elpidios lifted the bag to gage the weight of it.

'This is more than usual,' Elpidios happily said.

'Father, I am the best negotiator in Paphos, but it helps when I am selling the best olives on the Island,' Neilos said.

'My dream was to sell these olives all over Cyprus but unfortunately God has dealt me a cruel blow with my health, so it is now for you my son to continue the family tradition.'

Neilos gave an unconvincing smile.

'Father, on the way back from Paphos I met four men, four soldiers, one of them has a serious wound and I brought them back to the village, but they need three horses so they can rejoin their troops.'

'Soldiers from which army?' His father asked.

'They are soldiers from England and France fighting the Muslims in the Holy Land.'

'These soldiers are here to take our land,' Elpidios said raising his voice.

'Father, they are not. They want to capture Isaac Komnenos,'

'Do you not understand if they capture Komnenos they capture the whole Island. They fight in the name of our God, but they are nothing but murderers and pillages.'

Neilos turned his back on his Father.

'They fight in the name of God against the infidals, these men are sacrificing their lives to capture the holy city of Jerusalem and return it to Christianity,' Neilos said raising his voice.

Elpidios stood up.

'I care not who they are or who they represent I do not want these men in my village.'

'Give them horses and they will leave,' Neilos pleaded with his Father.

'Let me speak to some of my men about the horses. Go and tell them to stay put until I deal with it,' Elpidios told his son.

Phocus was still pacing up and down in the old mosque, Phillipe, Robert and Jalan were sleeping on the floor. Phillipe's arm was heavily strapped and in a new sling. The door creaked open and Neilos came in carrying a bag. Phocus rushed over to him.

'Have you managed to get the horses?' he asked Neilos.

'My father is going to get you horses.'

'When?' Pressed Phocus.

'Soon. I have bought you bread and cheese,' Neilos said opening the bag and placing the contents on a cloth on the floor. Phocus sat down and broke off a piece of bread. Neilos poured a small jar of olive oil into a container and sat next to him.

'Dip the bread in the oil,' said Neilos.

Phocus felt obliged and dipped the bread into the oil before eating. He nodded his head in approval before breaking another piece of bread and this time leaving it in the container to soak up the oil.

'When will you go to the Holy land?' Neilos asked.

Phocus waited until he had fully swallowed the bread.

'Once we capture Komnenos and the Island the plan is to set sail to Acre,' said Phocus.

'Do you not fear for your life?' Neilos asked.

'I have no fear as my life is to serve god and his son Jesus Christ. I joined King Richard's army in Sicily, after I helped capture Messina. Like many others being able to go on the crusade was my destiny,' Phocus explained.

'What do your family think of you joining the crusade?' Neilos asked inquisitively.

'My father and mother are both dead and I am not married, so I only have myself to care for. One day I hope to find a wife and start a family god willing. But first I must serve my Lord.'

Neilos found Phocus fascinating.

'I have had many dreams about leaving the village and leaving Cyprus, travelling to far distant lands to discover adventure, but in reality I live here and I sell my father's olives. I also do not know how I would feel leaving my Family. I love them and always will but there comes a crossroads in your life when you need to decide on the path you go down,' Neilos opened up.

'As far as I can see you have a good life here, a family who care for you and you care about them. Why would you want to leave?' Phocus asked.

'I agree with you, but I will never fulfil my dreams of adventure if I stay here for the rest of my life. What if I traveled to the Holy land and help reclaim Jerusalem for the whole of Christendom? Neilos asked.

Phocus laughed and bit into a large piece of goat's chesse.

'You are not a soldier, you have no combat experience, how would you survive?' Phocus said dismissing Neilos' dream.

Neilos stood to his feet.

'Can I take your crossbow and show you what I can do with it?' He asked Phocus.

Phocus stood and handed Neilos his crossbow and an arrow.

'Come,' Neilos urged Phocus and somewhat reluctantly he followed Neilos out of the building. Neilos stood on the path and pointed to the large cedar tree some one hundred yards away.

'Can you see the hollow in the middle of the tree trunk,' he asked Phocus, who nodded his head in confirmation. 'That is my target,' Neilos said confidently. He placed the bolt on the crossbow and pulled back the bow, before raising it and aiming at the tree. Neilos pulled the trigger and in a blink of Phocus' eye the bolt had landed plum in between the hollow in the cedar tree. Phocus was taken by surprise by the accuracy of Neilos' shot. Neilos handed Phocus the crossbow. 'Can you get anywhere near my arrow? Neilos laid down the challenge.

This put Phocus in a quandary. Decline the challenge and he would look like a coward in the eyes of Neilos, accept it and fail to get close to Neilos' bolt would be even more embarrassing. Phocus held out his hand and Neilos placed a bolt in his sweaty palm and without hesitation placed it in the crossbow, took aim and fired, the bolt landed approximately an inch or two above Neilos' arrow.

'You are good,' Neilos said with a sarcastic twist.

Phocus laughed and put his arms around Neilos.

'We could do with a marksman like you in the Holy Land,' Phocus said.

'Are you serious?'

'Archers are a rare commodity, good archers even rarer. I am a good archer and good with the sword, but the crusader armies require more and better archers.'

'Do you think I could be an archer in the army?' Neilos asked.

'If you can produce that kind of accuracy on the battlefield you could join the army tomorrow, but as I mentioned already my concern is you might be too young to go into battle,' Phocus said trying to deter him. 'Anyway, no one will be leaving this village if we do not find some horses.'

Neilos nodded his head.

'My Father is going to help you I will go back home and find out when he will deliver the horses.'

'Thank you again for helping, you have been akin to an angel,' Phocus said putting his hand on Neilos' shoulder.

A sense of urgency surged through Neilos' veins as he ran towards his house. On the way his thoughts turned him into a crusader running through the gates of Jerusalem and into the hordes of Muslim warriors waiting for him. Back in reality more than twenty horses were tied up outside his house. From his house, emerged his father followed by twenty men all carrying arms.

'No!' screamed Neilos in his head.

Elpidios was animated in his orders to the men.

'These men are enemies to our people, and we cannot allow them to take our Island,' he shouted at the top of his voice. 'We must eradicate their presence in Cyprus.'

The leader of the group, Gregorious, had long flowing hair and a long but neat beard. Holding his sword, he beckoned the others.

'I am a friend of Komnenos and any enemy of him is an enemy of mine,' Gregorious said with passion.

'And me, and me, and me, and me…,' came the response from each of the other men.

The men mounted their horses and rode towards the old mosque. Elpidios raised his hand to wish them luck.

Midday in the village was a quiet time as most of the farmers would head home to shelter from the intense sun and heat for a few hours. The endless sound of the crickets were punctured by the sound of horse hooves echoing through the village. The men arrived at the old mosque and dismounted from their horses.

'Half go around the back,' ordered Gregorious as he took out his sword. Ten men ran around to the back of the building while Gregorious and the others waited by the front door. They waited for a minute before Gregorious stormed in wielding his sword and screaming at the top of his voice, but he stopped in his tracks when he realised that there was no one there.

'Where are they?' Gregorious shouted.

Apart from the vases of olives the building was empty.

'Search in between the vases and the other rooms,' ordered Gregorious who was left deflated by the anti-climax and wandered outside, noticing that the horse belonging to Phocus was still tied to the gate.

'No one in the building,' one of the men said as the others from the back joined them.

'But they have no horses so they must be on foot,' stated Gregorious. 'We will leave the horses here and spilt up into two groups, one group will search the upper village and the other the lower end.'

A group of villagers had gathered outside the building and Gregorious marched up to them looking very menacing.

'Has anyone seen four soldiers?'

'Yes,' said an old man.

'Where are they?'

'In that building behind,' the old man said pointing to the old mosque.

'Thank you,' said Gregorious rolling his eyes and walking away.

Sunset was closing in and Gregorious walked forlornly towards Elpidios' house, the heat had taken its toll and he collapsed to his knees by the stream and dipped his head in the water. He struggled to his feet made his way the few hundred yards to the house. Elpidios was sat outside the house with Neilos.

'I am sorry Elpidios but the soldiers have gone. We searched the village and a couple of the men rode out to the mountain path but no sign of them,' explained Gregorious looking at Neilos.

Elpidios turned and looked at Neilos in a quizzical way.

'They would not have left without horses. What was the last conversation you had with them?'

'I said to them that I would speak to you about supplying them with horses and then I left,' Neilos said to his father.

'Well, if they have gone then that is good at least and no blood has been spilled in the village, but just keep your eyes open,' Elpidios told Gregorious.

A humid night air set in making it an uncomfortable night's sleep for the villagers and forcing many of them to abandon their homes to sleep outside. The stream was tranquil, and a gentle breeze blew through the branches of the trees and a full moon lit the village and surrounding lands providing ample light to see. Neilos drifted in and out the trees carrying a sheepskin bag tied around his back. Running through the trees brought back memories of his childhood, chasing his father, and playing hide and seek. When he was ten years old and with the help of his father he built a small wooden hut from dead olive trees. The hut was in between two trees and was surrounded with different types of plant shrubs so from a distance the hut was not visible. Neilos and his friends would use it as a secret hideout and would bring his various girlfriends there for fun and games. Scanning the fields to make certain no person was in sight he opened the door to the hut. Sat on the floor were the four crusaders.

'Where have you been?' asked Phillipe rather annoyed.

'I had to wait until everyone had gone to sleep,' Neilos explained while opening his bag. 'I have some lamb, beans and bread.'

'No wine?' asked Phocus.

Neilos placed the food on the floor.

'No wine, just water,' confirmed Neilos.

All four men dived into the food in particular the lamb.

'My father and Gregorious believe you have fled the village, but it is still not safe, so you need to stay put until I can get you out.'

The men were too busy eating to take part in any conversation.

'I can not get the horses for you,' Neilos admitted.

'What are we expected to do? Wait here?' Phocus said angrily.

Phillipe used his good arm to push himself up onto his feet.

'I have an idea we can take the boy's cart.'

Neilos, firstly did not like being referred to as a boy and secondly did not like the prospect of losing his cart.

'No, you can not take my cart,' he pleaded.

'Let us be rational about this,' Phocus said. 'If we take the cart where will we go? We do not know this Island so we will be traveling blind,' he continued.

'What do you suggest?' asked Robert.

'I can take you.'

The men all looked at each other before averting their gazes towards the direction of Neilos.

'Take us where?' questioned Phocus.

'Your men are heading to Nicosia. I know the roads so I can take you there by the coastal paths avoiding the forest and the mountains. If you go on your own you will be lost and even fall into the hands of Komnenos,' Neilos explained to them.

Phillipe nodded his head in approval, Robert shrugged his shoulders and Jalen looked at Phocus trying to gage his view.

'What would you say to your father?' Phocus asked.

'I will not tell him,' came Neilos' quick reply.

'The boy has a point. If we tried to reach Nicosia on our own, we might find our way somehow, but our army could depart thinking we are dead,' Phillipe said. 'I do not think we have any other choice.'

'Do we trust him?' Robert asked looking straight at Neilos.

'I for one trust him,' confirmed Phocus.

After a silent pause Robert put his arm around Neilos.

'Are you sure you want to do this?' Phocus asked. 'It could drive a wedge between you and your father.'

'I am happy to do this. I will have to deal with my father when the time comes,' Neilos said. 'I must go and prepare Zeus for the journey. We must leave just before sun rise before the villagers get up.'

'Go, be as quick as possible,' Phocus urged him.

The noise of the creaking stable door was loud enough to wake up Zeus the horse from his slumber. He did not seem best pleased as Neilos led him out and attached him to the cart. Neilos went into the house and tiptoed into his room. He wrapped some garments into a bundle and from underneath his bed he pulled out his crossbow and half a dozen metal tipped arrows. Before he left, he delved into a large clay pot and produced a bag of coins from it before rushing out of his room. A raid of the pantry uncovered some bread and he tied this up in a cloth and with both hands full he had to engage his elbow to open the door. Sounds of cockerels echoed through the village and this hastened Neilos as the sound was the village alarm call. Everything he was carrying was flung into the back of the cart and covered with a large sheepskin cover. It was far too early for Zeus but with the encouragement of Neilos on the reins the old horse began to trudge his way through the olive trees towards the wooden hut where the soldiers were hiding. The sun began to rise from behind the Troodos mountains in the distance and a certain amount of panic was etched on Neilos' face as time was against him to get the men out of the village before anyone noticed. Progress was slow as the rough terrain of the field proved difficult for Zeus and the cart until they finally pulled up outside the hut. The four men were ready and climbed into the back of the cart.

'Get under the cover until we leave the village,' Neilos instructed, and the men pulled it over them.

The ground was too rough to continue through the field so the only option Neilos had was to turn back, go past his house and take the path through the village and out. Once the cart made it back onto the path and with the sun now on Zeus' back, he began to trot. Neilos lowered his head as he rode past his house. Neilos navigated the cart through the village, passing the old mosque.

'What happened to my horse?' Phocus asked.

'I do not know, maybe Gregorious and his men took it,' came the answer from Neilos.

As the cart was leaving the village, a man was walking down the path and as the cart drew nearer Neilos recognized him, it was Tymous, one of the men who rode with Gregorious.

'Where are going this early in the morning, Neilos?'

Neilos did not stop.

'I am going to Polis to sell some olives,' he shouted out as he rode past him.

Tymous stood and watched the cart for a minute before he continued on his way.

'Stay under the cover, that was one of Gregorious' men,' Neilos told the men.

The cart made it's way on the spiral road to the port town of Polis.

'You can come out, all is clear,' Neilos told the men.

'My god it is hot under there,' Phocus complained while wiping the sweat off his forehead. 'Is this the road to Nicosia?' he asked.

'No, this road takes us to Polis. We will then take the coastal road to Morphou and then across the plains to Nicosia. This route avoids the forest and the mountains,' Neilos explained.

Robert and Phillipe nodded to each other in approval of Neilos' proposed route.

'How long will it take us to get to Nicosia?' Jalen asked Neilos.

'We will get there some time tonight, it will probably be darkness when we reach there,' Neilos replied.

They reached Polis and Neilos pulled up Zeus by a water well.

'Time to stretch our legs,' Phocus said as all four men jumped off the cart. Neilos took the bucket tied to the side of the cart and filled it with water from the well and placed it in front of Zeus. He also had a set of four small cups that he filled with water and handed them out to the men. Neilos also filled up two vases with water and put them in the back of the cart.

'I need a call of nature,' Jalan announced to everyone.

'Go behind those bushes,' Phocus said.

Jalan hurried along holding the side of his stomach and disappeared behind some bushes.

'Be careful of the snakes they may bite your bottom,' Neilos cheekily said making the other men laugh.

Some of the local inhabitants of the town started to gather round the men attracted by the crusader's distinct uniforms.

'We seem to have attracted quite a bit of attention,' Phocus said aloud.

'Jalan, are you nearly finished,' shouted Phillipe.

'Finished, I have only just started,' came the response back.

'Let us all get onto the cart and wait for him,' Phocus said beckoning the other men.

Minutes ticked by and still no sign of Jalan as a group of about ten men walked towards the cart.

'Jalan, hurry up man,' shouted Robert.

'Start going I will catch you up,' shouted back Jalan.

Zeus moved rapidly seemingly aware of the precarious situation they were all in. Before they knew it, the cart had sped away from the group of men.

'Slow down, we have to wait for Jalan,' Phillipe shouted out.

Neilos pulled the reins to slow down Zeus. They all looked back but there was no sight of Jalan.

'We must go back for him,' urged Phillipe as he yanked off the sling supporting his injured arm.

'No, let us wait here, he is big enough and strong enough to take care of himself,' Phocus said as Neilos stopped the cart.

They had waited for approximately ten minutes and Phillipe, who seemed anxious, jumped out of the cart.

'Where are you going?' Robert asked him.

'I am going back to find Jalan,'

'Get back in the cart,' demanded Phocus.

'Look,' shouted Neilos standing up on the seat of the cart pointing back. In the distanced they could see a figure of a person running towards them.

'Jalan!' Shouted Phillipe.

Neilos pulled down the reins and turned the cart around to the direction of Jalan. Seeing the cart coming towards him Jalan stopped running and waved at them.

'Good to see you again my brother,' Phocus said as he took Jalan's hand and pulled him onto the cart.

'What took you so long?' Phillipe asked Jalan as he shook his hand.

'I think I had too many of your olives Neilos.'

'Did you come across the group of men who began to follow us?' Phocus asked Jalan.

'Yes, that was an interesting encounter. They asked me where I came from and what I was doing on the Island. I told them I had to go and find my friends and walked away from them down the road. One or two them started shouting at me so I began to run, but two of them ran after me and I turned and laughed at them. I must have upset them. These two ran like greyhounds and caught me up so I punched them both to the ground and started to run again,' Jalan explained.

'Well, I think we should head out of this town as quickly as possible,' Phocus urged.

'Do not worry,' Neilos reassured them. 'We are heading on the coastal road now and this will take us all the way to Morphou,' he confirmed.

The men absorbed the breathtaking scenic view of the coast and clear blue sea. After a while they came across a sandy beach and decided that this would be a good spot for a break.

'I need a wash,' declared Jalan who promptly took off all his clothes and ran across the beach into the sea.

'That is a good idea,' Phillipe followed his friend but found the sand so hot that it burnt the soles of his feet. Soon, Phocus and Robert joined them while Neilos tended to Zeus giving him some fresh water and fruit before moving him under a tree to keep him in the shade.

'Neilos,' shouted Phocus, 'Why don't you come and join us, the sea is beautiful, so warm.'

Neilos smiled but was content just to sit down on the sand.

Suddenly Neilos jumped up in panic, his clothes soaked in water. Standing around him were the four men all laughing, Jalan placed the empty bucket next to Neilos. 'Don't worry you will be dry in five minutes in this heat,' said Phocus helping him up.

Neilos took off his wet clothes and hanged them on the side of the cart while the others were changing back into their clothes. Neilos changed into dry clothes when his attention was drawn to something moving in the distance. As he stared intently ten men on horses approached.

'We have company,' Neilos shouted to the others and they all ran back to the cart. The men on the horses rode onto the beach and up to the cart. Neilos and the men shielded themselves behind the cart.

'How can I help?' Neilos said to the men on the horses.

'Where are these men from?' One of the horsemen asked.

Phocus stepped out from behind the cart.

'We are from different lands and we are on route to the holy land to re-capture the holy city of Jerusalem from the Muslim infidels and deliver it back to our lord,' Phocus explained.

'What are you doing in our land?' The horseman asked in a hostile manner.

'I repeat we are just passing through your land, enjoying the beautiful views and we just jumped into the beautiful sea,' said Phocus trying to placate him.

'I hear that the English King is attempting to take over the Island,' the horseman countered.

'No, this is not the truth. We are not here to fight with our fellow Christian people. You are our brothers,' said Phocus smiling and holding out his arms.

The horseman nodded and turned back and gesticulated to the others to head back. The horsemen rode off the beach and onto the road and back in the direction they came from. Neilos breathed a sigh of relief.

'Men I think we should go now,' recommended Neilos. Everyone got back onto the cart and Zeus tiptoed onto the Road and to everyone's surprise he trotted off.

'Come on Zeus, go, go, go,' Neilos bellowed out.

Zeus picked up a good steady pace as the cart hugged the rough undulating coastal road. The relentless sun and heat had dried the men and their clothes and was now in the process of making them perspire.

'Look, behind us,' Phillipe said from the back of the cart. Neilos stopped the cart and looked down the winding road and in the distance, he could see men on horseback coming up the road behind them. Phocus stood up on the cart to get a better view.

'I think it is same men who spoke to us on the beach,' Phocus confirmed.

'What do they want from us now?' Asked Jalan.

'I would guess that they do not want to have a pleasant conversation,' speculated Phillipe.

The men in pursuit carried an array of weapons, most had swords but a couple were carrying maces, these deadly weapons were made of wood while the ball was made of iron. One of the men had a double-headed axe, the most lethal of all weapons. As they turned around one of the sharp corners, the cart came into view and encouraged by this, all ten men grasped and raised their weapons, their intent quite clear, but as they approached the cart they found it empty. They circled the cart, but Zeus seemed unfazed by all the commotion happening around him. One of the horsemen rode up to the cart and pulled up the sheepskin cover, suddenly from under the cover rose Jalen and with one swing of his axe he decapitated the horseman. From behind a rock Phocus jumped out and aiming his crossbow fired the bolt straight through the neck of another horseman. Neilos appeared from behind a tree on higher ground and using his crossbow and with pinpoint accuracy fired it at a horseman, the impact of the bolt knocked the horseman off his horse. Robert and Philippe charged the remaining horsemen knocking two of them off their horses, Jalan leapt off the cart onto two of the horsemen before running them through with his sword. Carnage ensued thereafter and after about five minutes the bodies of the Cypriot horsemen lay strewn over the road. Phocus, Jalan and Robert rounded up four of the horses and Phillipe collected all the weapons from the dead men and put them into the cart. All ten of the bodies were dragged to the side of the road and lay side by side. Jalan crossed himself as a blessing to the dead men.

'We better get going before any of their friends come looking for them,' said Phocus. 'I will ride on one of the horses.'

Jalan and Robert mounted horses while Philippe sat next to Neilos on the cart.

'Move on Zeus,' Phocus urged the horse.

The cart led the way and Phocus, Jalan and Robert followed on horseback.

'The boy did good,' proclaimed Robert to Phocus, 'He is a good marksman. He could be useful on the battlefields of the Holy Land.'

'I know, we have spoken about it, but he is only sixteen,' Phocus said.

'Sixteen is the age when a boy becomes a man, he just killed a man so by my reckoning he has just become that man,' Robert said, 'If he wants to join our crusade, we should recommend him to the King,' he concluded.

Phocus nodded his head in agreement.

They entered the town of Morphou stopping by a stream to replenish their water supply. Neilos walked into the market square and bought bread, goats' cheese and small cucumbers that were grown locally. In the back of his mind, he could still see the image of the horseman's face as the arrow entered him. That event added to the time spent with the men and the bond he had developed with them had convinced him that his future lay away from his village. He knew that once they reached Nicosia, a life changing decision had to be made. Realistically, he had two options, once he had guided the men to Nicosia he could turn back and return to the village or he could join their army and travel to the Holy Land. He headed back to the men and once again they had attracted the attention of the locals, but the locals seemed far more friendly than the locals were in Polis. Jalan was entertaining the children with his juggling skills whilst Phillipe and Robert were trying to converse with the local girls. Phocus kept his eye on everyone aware that the situation could change from hospitable to hostility in seconds. Neilos put the goods he had purchased into the cart.

'We should leave now if we are to make Nicosia before night fall,' Neilos said to Phocus.

'Men, we have to leave,' Phocus barked out.

Phillipe and Robert reluctantly said goodbye to the girls and Jalan gave the fruit he was juggling to the children.

'I like this place,' Jalan admitted to the others.

'Very friendly people,' Phillipe said as he waived goodbye to the girl he was talking to who waived back at him.

Phocus, Jalan and Robert mounted their horses as Neilos and Phillipe climbed onto the cart and off they set. The road from Morphou to Nicosia was a straight route along the plains and just under twenty nine miles in distance.

Zeus set a good pace and the three men on horseback had to encourage their horses to keep up with the cart.

Buildings started to appear far in the distance.

'Are we near?' Phocus asked.

'Yes, you can see the city in the distance,' replied Neilos.

They passed some carts that were traveling in the opposite direction. Reaching the outskirts of Nicosia, farmers were tending to their lands as they rode past the first houses. Before long they reached the East gate of the City and into sight came the large banner draped over the top of the gate. It was the royal banner of King Richard. Robert and Jalan rode on towards the gate to show the guards that they were wearing the same insignia.

'Where have you come from?' asked one the guards.

'We were riding with Guy de Lusignan and we got detached from the rest of the men after being ambushed by some local fighters,' Jalan explained.

The guards opened the gate.

'We captured the city with little resistance,' the guard said, 'but Komnenos and some of his men escaped and headed East. Lusignan has gone in pursuit of him. Ride into the center, the King has just arrived.'

The men headed into the hustle and bustle of the center of the city. The locals were in a state of flux following the arrival of the crusaders. A soldier directed Neilos and the men into the square where the soldiers had congregated. Neilos tied Zeus next to a watering trough with the other horses and followed the others.

'You!' shouted a solider pointing at Neilos, 'Where are you going?' the soldier asked.

Phillipe turned back and put his hand on Neilos' shoulder.

'He is with us,' Phillipe said to the soldier.

The crowd of crusaders waited with anticipation. Neilos looked around, he had never seen a crowd this large and this raucous.

'What is everyone waiting for?' Neilos asked Phillipe.

'That man over there,' Phillipe said pointing vaguely to another crowd of men. Neilos was confused but then the noise steadily turned to silence. A wooden cart was wheeled into the center of the square becoming a makeshift platform. A knight climbed on top of the cart. He was tall, well-built and wore a beard, over his golden chainmail he wore a red surcoat that was embroidered with three golden lions and a golden crown. Neilos nudged Phillipe and he turned to him.

'King Richard,' Phillipe whispered to him.

'Fellow men, fellow knights, fellow crusaders, today we have conquered this Island,' the King was interrupted by huge cheers and roars from the crowd. 'The traitor Komnenos has been captured,' the King continued but once again he was interrupted with choruses of cheers, 'so our objective has been archived. I urge all men to return to Lemesos and we will set sail to the Holy Land in four days, but in the meantime, I grant you three days of freedom, enjoy,' he bellowed out and this led to more cheering. The King then jumped off the cart and made his way through the throng of soldiers but stopped when he saw Phocus, Robert, Jalan and Phillipe standing together and approached them before hugging and shaking their hands. 'My brothers, for the grace of god, I was told that you were killed,' the King said to them before looking at Neilos. 'Who is this?' he asked.

'He saved our lives your highness, he is a warrior, and he would like to serve under you on the crusade,' Phocus said to the King.

The King starred into Neilos' eyes. Neilos looked up into his grey eyes, his red hair protruding out of his crown. 'You must be a warrior if you saved the lives of my brothers. I would be proud if you served in my army,' the King said to Neilos.

'It would be an honour for me to serve your royal highness in the Holy land,' Neilos replied and the King shook his hand.

'My brothers will look after you, we set sail in four days, a day after my wedding,' he said while continuing his foray through the crowd.

Neilos' eyes followed King Richard through the mass of knights and realized that this short conversation had changed the course of his life.

FIVE

Terra, 1570

The heat from the furnace was intense and added to the air temperature of nearly forty five degrees Celsius. It was almost unbearable for the ironsmith, named Bedros, to stand for too long near the forge, but he had no option. He was already well behind in fulfilling the order of making one hundred swords, each with the specification of being double-edged, straight bladed and a blade length of thirty inches. In total with the one-handed cruciform with pommel added, the length of the sword would be thirty five inches. Standard use for Venetian soldiers. Maximos, his assistant, turned up in the nick of time.

'Good you are here. We need to finish off five more swords by midday,' Bedros said in a panic.

'But we have until the end of the day to deliver them, do we not?' questioned Maximos.

'No, I have to deliver all the swords to the garrison at Akourdaleia by midday, every hour that I am late they will deduct two ducats from the payment and I will get the blame.'

'I understand,' Maximos said picking up the tongs ready to transport the metal piece from the forge to the anvil. Bedros placed his sword into a slack tub of water to cool it down and moved onto the next piece of metal. Within an hour the men had completed the five swords. Bedros used a rag to wipe down the sword before he used a metal file and then a stone to sharpen the blade, whilst Maximos loaded the cart with the swords. The blades were so sharp he had to use a large cloth to carry them to avoid lacerations to his hands and forearms.

'I have loaded them all,' Maximos told Bedros.

'Let us go,' Bedros said aloud before climbing onto the cart followed by Maximos.

'We need to go to Synglitico's house first to collect olive oil he is sending to the garrison.'

Giovanni Synglitico was instructing two of his workers on watering the olive trees on his land as Bedros and Maximos arrived into the courtyard.

'Help put the olive oil jars into the cart,' Giovanni instructed his workers.

The men loaded twelve jars of olive oil onto the cart, while Giovanni examined the swords.

'Bedros, I must commend you on your workmanship, the blades on these are so sharp they will cut through any Turk,' Giovanni said.

'These are the best I have ever made,' Bedros proudly said.

'Make sure you count the money they give you, two hundred and twenty five ducats, no deductions. Their minds are thinking about the Turkish invasion and not money matters. Ask the garrison captain if they are going to stay at Akourdaleia. Now be gone,' Giovanni said slapping the behind of the cart horse.

Bedros had no time to reply as the horse shot off. The workers made haste to the olive groves leaving Giovanni standing alone in the courtyard. He walked to the entrance of the courtyard taking in the view of his lands and beyond.

'If only I could read your thoughts,' came a voice from behind that startled him. It was his wife, Maria.

'What are you pondering about,' Maria asked.

'Our future,' he said.

'There is nothing to ponder about. We are leaving and there is nothing more we can discuss,' she said bluntly.

'Walk with me to the church,' he said grabbing her hand and setting off up the path towards the church. 'God the almighty will enlighten us.'

'There is nothing God can tell us that we do not already know. The Turks are going to invade any day so we must leave the Island. There is a ship leaving Paphos for Venice in two days and we must be on it,' she said adamantly.

'Do you not think we should stay and defend the Island?' he asked.

'How long do you believe our army could defend the Island?' she countered.

'I asked my question first,' he said sarcastically.

'If we had a chance then yes, but the Turkish army is far superior, if we stay, we face certain death, not just us but also our children. Then the answer to your question is no.'

'My answer is the same as yours. In the end the Turks will defeat the Venetians.'

'So, what is there to think about? The only option is to leave,' she said.

'All this land,' Giovanni said pointing in the general direction. 'All our land, what will become of it?' Posing the question to Maria.

'You must forget this land. If we add the payment from the garrison to our savings, we will have aplenty, we can buy land in Venice and beyond. There is no future on this Island.'

Giovanni looked at her, in his heart of hearts he knew she was right.

'I admit we must do what is right for our children and ensure that they have a safe home,' he said as they approached the church.

'Do we need to go in?' Maria asked.

'The door is open; it would be impolite if we did not enter.'

Inside the Church was probably the coolest building in the village, and most villagers would enter to escape the harsh temperatures outside rather than to pray. At the back, in the corner, was a statue. On the floor was a plaque with an inscription in Latin. It read NEILOS ARGOMOS, 1175 – 1192, KNIGHT WHO DIED IN THE HOLY LAND FIGHTING IN THE CRUSADE.

'He was so young,' Maria said.

'Nearly four hundred years later and we are still fighting Muslims,' Giovanni exclaimed.

The Venetian army garrison at Akourdaleia was a hundred strong and as Bedros and Maximos arrived, the troops were in the middle of evacuating the fort.

'Where is the Captain?' Bedros asked one of the soldiers.

'Over there,' the solider said pointing to a group of men sat on the fort steps. The pair walked over and caught the eye of the garrison commander, Captain Pomanto.

'Welcome, you have brought the new swords,' he said jumping up with an abundance of enthusiasm. 'I must inspect them,' the Captain said walking over to the cart.

'Are you leaving?' Bedros asked the Captain.

'Have you not heard the news?' he said leaving the pair behind as he forged ahead to view the swords.

'No,' replied Bedros as the Captain pulled off the cover on the cart to reveal the sword, lifting one up to inspect it.

'What news?' asked Bedros.

The Captain was too preoccupied admiring the sword, the sun caught the glistening metal and the reflection made him squint his eyes. Holding the sword, he began doing slashing and thrusting actions making Bedros and Maximos jump out the way.

'Perfect weight,' the Captain uttered, 'and you have one hundred of them?'

'Yes, and we also have twelve jars of olive oil as well. Sorry Captain, you mentioned hearing about the news.'

'The Turks landed on the Island two days ago, and all regiments have been ordered to fortify Nicosia, Kyrenia and Famagusta. We have been assigned to Nicosia,' the Captain explained.

'How many Turks are there?' Maximos asked.

'Far too many, they say thousands.'

Bedros and Maximos looked at each other in panic while the Captain ordered a couple of the soldiers to unload the swords and olive oil and load it onto a large six-wheel cart.

'How long will it take the Turks to reach Nicosia?' Bedros asked the Captain.

'If the Turks can mass their soldiers without any opposition and allowed to march directly to Nicosia, it will be a matter of days. We should be able to defend Nicosia until reinforcements arrive.'

Bedros and Maximos strolled back to their cart as the Captain wandered off, but he turned to see the pair waiting by the cart and rushed back to them.

'Are you are waiting for payment?' The Captain asked the men.

'Yes, two hundred and twenty five ducats for the swords and olive oil,' Bedros confirmed.

Giovanni was wandering through the olive trees still trying to come to terms with the idea that he would be leaving all this behind. The village of Terra was given to his great-grandfather by the King of Cyprus over a century ago and the thought that soon it would fall into the hands of the Turks appalled him. His thoughts were interrupted by the sight of soldiers on horseback approaching his house. He recognized the red tunics as being uniforms of the Venetian army.

'Good day,' Giovanni greeted the soldiers.

'Good morning Sir, my men and I have come from the garrison at Paphos. Can we rest our horses and drink water from the stream?' the Captain of the troops asked Giovanni.

'Please be my guests, this is my land, so feel free to graze your horses here,' he replied.

'Thank you, kind Sir,' the Captain said as he dismounted his horse, approached Giovanni, and shook his hand. 'My name is Lorenzo Tiepolo, Captain of the Paphos garrison.'

'I am Giovanni Synglitico.'

'Synglitico. You must be related to Commander Zegno,' said Tiepolo.

'He is my uncle.' Giovanni confirmed.

'And Tommaso Synglitico, Viscount of Nicosia?' Tiepolo asked.

'He is my Father.'

Captain Tiepolo bowed his head in honour.

'I apologise if I treated you with disrespect in asking for my men to rest on your land.'

'Captain Tiepolo you can relax, there is no need for such formalities. Why have you abandoned Paphos? Is there not a ship departing from there in two days heading to Venice?' Giovanni asked with curiosity.

'The port is closed, that ship has sailed and all ships leaving the Island are now departing from Famagusta. All Venetian military have been ordered to abandon their garrisons and head to the main cities by your Uncle. We are going to Famagusta,' Tiepolo told Giovanni.

'I do not understand, soldiers should have headed to Lemesos and attacked the Turks as they landed,' said an animated Giovanni.

'I am paid to follow the orders of my commanders. I believe the strategy is to fortify the main garrisons and hold the Turks at bay until the reinforcements arrive from Venice,' Tiepolo said.

'Be honest with me Captain, if reinforcements do not arrive, how long can the Island survive?'

'The only city that can survive for a long period of time is Famagusta. The fortifications there are far stronger than Nicosia,' the Captain said with honesty.

'My Father, Uncle and cousins are in Nicosia,' said a concerned Giovanni as the Captain nodded his head.

'Let us pray to god that Venice sends help soon, we must keep faith and hope,' said the Captain.

'My wife and I had planned to take the ship from Paphos to Venice. Her family is Venetian, and we want to take our children there.'

'That would be a wise move, but I do not know if any ships will leave Famagusta, especially now the Turkish Navy have ships in the waters around the Island,' warned the Captain.

The conversation was making Giovanni nervous.

'Captain, my number one priority is the safety of my family. What would you do in my situation?'

'I would take my family to Famagusta, that way we can hold out for reinforcements or hope for ships to arrive and evacuate women and children, but if this was my land, I would not want to abandon it, so I would stay and defend it as long as humanly possible,' Captain Tiepolo's thoughts echoed those held by Giovanni and watching Maria and his three children walking towards them cemented his view and the decision he was going to make.

'Captain, would you escort my wife and children to Famagusta?' Giovanni asked.

'It would be my pleasure,' Captain Tiepolo said out loud.

Giovanni approached Maria and his children and started talking to them.

Darkness descended as Bedros and Maximos arrived back to the village. Groups of villagers were walking towards the church and Maximos recognized a couple of his neighbours.

'Where is everyone going?' Maximos asked.

'Synglitico has summoned the whole village to the church,' one of the old farmers replied.

Inside the church Giovanni and the priest, Father Yionnis, waited as the villagers entered. The last people to arrive were Bedros and Maximos who closed the door behind him.

'I must let everyone know that the Turks have landed in Cyprus. The Venetian army will defend the Island, but they have abandoned the towns and villages. Soon the Turks will arrive and take our lands, so it is up to us not only to defend Terra but to inflict as much damage to the Turkish army as possible. This will mean it will generate more time for the Venetian army to defend the Island until reinforcements arrive from Venice. We must remember that the Venetians are invades themselves and that this Island of Cyprus belongs to us, us the Cypriots,' said Giovanni, his voice echoing through the church. 'I believe Father Yionnis would like to say a few words,' he beckoned the priest forward.

'We are all children of God and protectors of the almighty,' he said picking up a cross from the altar, 'if we do not protect our people or our land, these invaders will not only burn all our crosses, but they will burn all our families. We must therefore protect Christ, the lord and our people,' Father Yionnis preached as he stepped back, and Giovanni stepped forward.

'Therefore, I call on everyone present to help defend the village. Could anyone who would like to defend their land please raise their hands?' Giovanni asked.

Bedros and Maximos rushed forward towards Giovanni and the priest with their hands raised.

'We will fight the Turks,' shouted Bedros.

This reaction spurred everyone else to stand and raise their hands.

'Fight the Turk, fight the Turk, fight the Turk,' sang the throng in the church, the sound escaping out and heard throughout the village.

Bedros and Maximos had spent all night in front of the forge, producing dozens of crossbow bolts, axe heads, and breast plates. Giovanni put his saddle onto the horse and strapped in his sword and axe onto the saddle. The sound of galloping horses disturbed the peaceful tranquility as a group of forty or so men on horseback rode into his courtyard. Giovanni smiled to express his surprise at the number of men that had turned up. Closer inspection of one of the men revealed the bearded features of the Priest, Father Yionnis.

'Father, what are you doing here?' asked Giovanni.

The Priest dismounted.

'I will do whatever is humanly possible to protect Christ the lord and if that means entering into battle with other men, so be it.'

'I understand your reasoning Father, but the best way you can serve God is to stay here and attend to the people. There will be a large amount of people concerned and you are the one person in the village who people can trust and respect,' said Giovanni urging him to stay.

'Every hand helps in battle so I hope I can make a difference,' Father Yionnis said.

'Father, I can not stop you and you need to do whatever God deems,' stated Giovanni.

'It is the will of God,' the Priest said.

'So be it,' Giovanni said holding out his hand and the Priest shook it. At that moment Bedros arrived with his cart, followed a minute or so later by Maximos on horseback, also leading Bedros' horse. The cart contained a wide array of weapons and each man had their choice of weapon.

'Men, have a look in that box,' Giovanni said pointing to large wooden box on the ground.

Some of the men wandered over and lifted the cloth covering the box. They were taken aback by the contents, a collection of muskets, pistols, and a couple of kegs of gunpowder.

'Gifts from the Venetian soldiers,' Giovanni said, 'first come first serve.' This led to a rush to the box. Giovanni quickly went back into the house to find his lucky charm. A gold roman coin dating back to the reign of Hadrian that he found near the stream when he was a boy. He rubbed it and put in the pocket of his tunic, and his thoughts turned to Maria and his children, and their safety. By now they would have reached Famagusta. How long would it be before he set eyes on them again? It was a question he did not have an answer to.

The band of men left the village and headed towards Paphos, some twenty miles away. One of the men was carrying a banner. A blue cross on a white background. Giovanni was fascinated by this and kept looking back at the banner.

'Didosys, what are you carrying?' Giovanni asked.

'It depicts the cross of Christ floating towards heaven to represent all Cypriots,' explained Didosys.

'I would be proud to fight under that flag,' Giovanni admitted.

Bedros and Maximos rode ahead to conduct a reconnaissance of the road leading into Paphos. It was eerily quiet as the pair entered the Town and headed towards the harbour, and to the ruins of the castle that the Venetian soldiers had dismantled using gunpowder before abandoning the town. They spotted a local man who was running carrying what looked like an anchor.

'Hello!' shouted Maximos.

The man stopped and walked towards them.

'Where is everyone?' Maximos asked the man.

'Hiding from the Turks. They are approaching from the east,' the man informed them.

'How far away are they?' Bedros asked him.

The man turned and looked up.

'Listen,' he said.

A sound of drums punctured the air.

'They are here,' the man said running off.

Bedros and Maximos mounted their horses and headed for higher ground overlooking the harbour. Maximos rode off to notify the others while Bedros hid behind a wall. The sound of the drums grew louder, a couple of children ran past Bedros probably trying to get home. The incessant sound drew nearer and nearer, and he was startled when he heard horse hooves behind him, but was relieved when it turned out to be Giovanni and the others.

'Can you see them?' asked Giovanni.

'No, but I can certainly hear them,' Bedros said.

Giovanni surveyed the scene and pointed below to the road parallel to the harbour that led to the castle.

'Maximos take a couple of men and push that cart to the middle of the road and turn it over,' Giovanni instructed.

'We could pour some gunpowder on it and explode it when they get close,' suggested Maximos.

'Good idea, take the men with the muskets, that way we can open fire from two positions,' Giovanni said.

Maximos led ten men down and they rolled the abandoned cart into the middle of the road before turning it over. Maximos opened the keg and poured gunpowder on the base of the cart and ran down the road pouring a line of the gunpowder ready to light. Three of the men loaded their muskets with lead balls and gunpowder, and took up positions behind the cart.

'Men be careful sparks from the guns do not ignite the gunpowder otherwise you will be shot into heaven,' Maximos shouted as he knelt behind a water trough. He signaled to Giovanni directly above him. Archers were positioned along the road above waiting in anticipation with their crossbows aimed to fire. The sound of the Turkish drums was virtually on top of them but still no soldiers were in sight.

'I see them, over there,' shouted one of the men as all eyes diverted to the direction he was pointing in. A group of Turkish soldiers on horseback, known as Akincis, rode into the center of the Town approaching the castle. They wore pointed helmets and chainmail on top of elaborate embroidered red and gold uniforms. They all carried bows and arrows on their backs.

'I count fifteen of them,' Father Yionnis said softly.

The Turks approached the castle but once they ascertained that it had been abandoned, they turned around. One of the Turkish soldiers was seen pointing towards the overturned cart and two of them rode towards it. Maximos had lit a torch in preparation. As the Turks approached the cart one of the Cypriots moved and was seen. The first Turk rapidly took his bow and arrow and prepared to fire it.

'Shoot!' yelled Maximos and before the Turk could take aim, he was shot off his horse. The second Turkish soldier turned and rode off. The other two men shot their muskets but failed to hit the fleeing soldier.

'Fall back,' shouted Maximos, and as the men behind the cart started running back the Turkish soldiers began firing arrows as they rode towards the cart. Maximos lit the trail of gunpowder and ran, and as the Turkish soldiers reached the cart an almighty explosion vibrated through the harbour and through the rest of the town.

'Fire at will,' Giovanni shouted, and the men fired with pistols and crossbows, but the smoke from the explosion obscured the view and they were just firing randomly. Maximos and the men ran up the winding road to reach the others. The smoke cleared to reveal bodies that lay strewn along the road, both human and equine.

'How many did we get?' asked Maximos.

'I can see eight bodies,' Bedros called out.

Father Yionnis crossed himself.

'I think we have overstayed our welcome in Paphos, so we better head back,' Giovanni said.

The men placed the pistols, muskets, and keg of gunpowder back into the cart. Father Yionnis noticed movement in the distance. Turkish soldiers maneuvered a large object into view.

'What is that?' asked the Father.

Giovanni stood next to the Father but could not enlighten him in identifying the object.

'It is a canon,' confirmed Bedros grabbing and pulling them back, 'we have to leave now,' and they began to run to their horses.

'A large bang shook the ground and was followed by a whistling sound and a spilt second later an explosion destroyed a building in front of them. Two of the Cypriots were blown off their horses as the rest rode through. Seconds later another canon ball hit a building turning it into rubble. Giovanni and Father Yionnis rode back and helped the two injured men by pulling them onto their horses before they rode out of the town.

Giovanni stood on the side of the port at Famagusta as the ship was leaving the harbour. On board was Maria and his three children, rigorously waving at their father. Giovanni shouted out.

'I will see you in Venice.'

Maria mouthed out 'I love you.' Venetian soldiers lined along the fortress walls of the city; on the west side they faced the Turkish army that had surrounded the city for months. Panic set in as one of the soldiers on lookout duty spotted a Turkish navy ship approaching the harbour. The Turkish ship began firing canons at the Venetian ship.

'Someone tell the Captain to turn back,' screamed Giovanni.

It was too late. The Venetian ship took three or four direct hits causing a fire to break out on the deck. Giovanni disregarding his pistol and sword jumped into the sea and began to swim towards the stricken ship but could see that the ship was listing badly. Two more direct hits sealed the ships fate and within seconds it began to sink. Giovanni started screaming then there was silence. He woke up in a cold sweat and it took him a few seconds to dispel his confusion and work out his bearings and recognise that the whole thing he had imagined had been a dream, well in essence a nightmare. He was laying in the shade under a tree near the roadside between Paphos and Terra. Father Yionnis was tending to the two injured men, one of them had a head injury and the Father wrapped it tightly with a cloth that he had torn from the cover of the cart. Some of the other men were engaging in horseplay.

'Save your energy for the Turks,' Bedros shouted out to them as he walked towards Giovanni.

'Did you enjoy your rest?' Bedros asked Giovanni.

'No, I wish I never fell asleep. Any sign of the Turks?'

'They are still in Paphos. Are they going to stay there?' Bedros asked.

'All roads lead to Nicosia. We should go there, my father, brothers and uncle are waiting, waiting for the inevitable, but I am torn whether to head straight to Famagusta. I want to see my wife and children and make sure they are safe,' Giovanni explained.

'I want to be honest with you Giovanni, the men have been talking and they want to head back to Terra and be with their families, just like you want to be with your family. We have given the Turks a bloody nose but that is the most we will be able to achieve.'

Giovanni pondered on Bedros' words.

'I will tell the men that we will return to the village. I will go to Nicosia to see my Father before going to Famagusta to be with my wife and children,' Giovanni said clear in his intentions.

The Villages greeted the returning men like heroes, they hugged and kissed the men. A huge barbeque was set up outside the church, and every household brought food and drink. The occasion was tinged with sadness for Giovanni as his wife and children were not there to greet him. He walked up to Bedros, who was playing with his children.

'I must go now,' Giovanni said as the two men embraced, 'enjoy the day and look after all the people.'

'Will I ever see you again my friend?' Bedros asked him.

'God willing,' answered Giovanni.

'Stay a bit longer,' Bedros said putting his hand on his shoulder.

'I need to go home and then set off to Nicosia.'

Everyone shook Giovanni's hand as he made his way through the people.

'Giovanni,' called someone from behind.

He turned back to see Father Yionnis walking towards him. The Father shook his hand.

'May God spare you and your family.'

'I hope so too,' came Giovanni's reply.

Giovanni washed and changed when he got home. Wanting to travel lightly he took a small amount of money, his pistol, and his sword. Wandering out into the fields he took one last view of this landscape, unsure if he would ever get the opportunity to take in this view again, but he had no time to dwell. His priority was to find his family. The temptation was to take the shortest journey through the forest and mountains, but the terrain would be too unpredictable, so he decided to head North on the coastal road to Morphou and then onto Nicosia. Passing the old town of Polis, he thought of something and rummaged through his pockets. Where was his roman coin? He stopped and searched his saddle but to no avail. He clinched his fist with anger as this would be the first time that he had left the village without the coin since he first found it as a child. It was too far into his journey to head back now, but for a minute or two he considered heading back to Terra. He continued but it kept nagging him in the back of the head.

'Damn it!' he shouted as he turned back and galloped back to the village.

Not wanting to be seen by anyone Giovanni tied his horse to a tree just outside the village and climbed down the hill, across the stream and into the fields of olive trees and walked towards his house. Approaching the house, he saw some men wandering around the courtyard, he hid behind a tree when he realised that he did not recognize the language they were talking in as it was not Greek or Italian. He heard two of the men approaching and a peek finally confirmed his suspicions, they were Turkish soldiers. Frustratedly, he lay flat on the ground behind the tree as his pistol and sword were still in the saddle on his horse. The soldiers turned and headed back to Giovanni's house picking olives off the trees along the way. His immediate instinct was to find a way to warn the other villagers but following the road through the village was out of the question, so the only alternative was to navigate across the stream, through the farms and climb up to reach the upper part of the village. Stealth like, Giovanni ascended the steep hill to reach the top of the village. A crowd had congregated outside the church and Giovanni attached himself to the back of crowd. Turkish soldiers all holding muskets stood in a line in front of the church. Then the Captain of the Turkish regiment stepped out accompanied by a Greek civilian, who acted as an interpreter. The Captain began to speak in Turkish and then stopped after a couple of sentences.

'We come in peace and our intentions are totally peaceful. We would like the whole village to continue just as normal,' the Greek interpreter bellowed out.

The Turkish captain spoke again but this time an ounce of anger was detected in his voice.

'But if anyone resists or confronts any of our soldiers, we will have no option but to deal with those people with a firm hand,' said the interpreter. The Captain continued gradually raising the tone of his voice.

'Unfortunately, a few of the villagers felt the need to oppose our soldiers,' the Captain nodded, and the line of soldiers opened, and a group of men all with their hands tied were led to the front. The group included Bedros, Maximos and Father Yionnis. The Captain approached the group and pulled out the Father and started speaking. 'The Sultan fully respects his subjects and respects their faith and who they worship. The Priest will be spared to continue his work at the Church and all worshipers will be allowed to attend church as normal,' Spoke the interpreter and one of the soldiers untied the Father's hands and pushed him towards the villagers. The Captain continued. Some of the villagers saw Giovanni and pulled him into the crowd.

'These others must be punished in line with the laws of Sultanate,' the interpreter said as the men were led to a clearing next to the church. Giovanni tried to push through the crowd but some of the villagers pulled him back. The six men were made to kneel, and the Captain signaled to Father Yionnis, who rushed forward to bless the men. A burley soldier appeared from no where carrying a large sword and walked over to the first man in line and in anticipation the men in the crowd shielded the women and children, as the soldier raised his sword and with one swift movement, he beheaded the man. Cries and screams reverberated off the church and other buildings of the village. Two more men were beheaded in quick succession leaving Father Yionnis trailing behind. Maximos was next. 'We must do something,' Giovanni shouted as he surged forward, this prompted the Turkish Soldiers to point their muskets at the crowd. Maximos was beheaded. Giovanni ran forward but the Captain drew his sword and thrust it towards Giovanni making him stop with the tip of the sword touching Giovanni's chest. The Captain shouted some words in Turkish. The interpreter walked up to Giovanni.

'Do you want to join them?
Giovanni, feeling helpless shook his head. The Captain pushed Giovanni back into the crowd by poking his sword at Giovanni's chest, who gave the Captain a cold hard stare straight into his eyes. The Captain just smiled at him. This interlude interrupted the flow of the executioner and made Bedros wait a few moments longer for his fate. Giovanni turned and walked away as the screams of the villagers confirmed Bedros' death.

A scene of devastation greeted Giovanni on the return to his home. The Turkish soldiers had gone but had ransacked the whole house. Furniture had been flung and broken vases and all glasses had been smashed and his clothes strewn all around. The whole purpose of his return was to find his roman coin but trying to find the garment he wore when he returned from Paphos in the sea of clothes would prove time consuming and time was not on his side. With Turkish solders swarming the area he needed to get to Nicosia before they blocked all roads into the city. He spotted the chainmail he had worn and still attached underneath was the tunic, he rushed over and searched the pocket, and a sudden sense of relief descended upon his face as he took the gold coin out. He examined the coin closely for Hadrian's head before putting it in the pocket of the tunic he was wearing. Giovanni opened the door and came face to face with Dareia, the old lady who cleaned the house.

'Dareia, I was not expecting you,' he said with surprise.
'I heard the Turks had gone through your house.'
He opened the door fully to show her the extent of the damage.
'I think it will take you a few days to clear this mess up, wait here,' he said as he walked outside to his horse and

took out some money from the saddle before walking back.

'Dareia, take this,' he said placing several coins in the palm of her hand. 'I would be grateful if you can clean as much as you can. I have to leave now.'

'Are you going to Nicosia?' she asked.

'Yes, I am going to see my Father and then I hope to go to Famagusta to meet up with Maria and the children.'

Dareia clinched his hand.

'May God protect you on the journey,' she said blessing him. 'The Turks have decreed that we bury the men who were executed this afternoon.'

'This afternoon?' Giovanni said with surprise.

'The soldiers will only leave once the funerals for the men have taken place and they are buried,' explained Dareia. 'Father Yionnis will ring the church bells to signal the beginning of the funerals.'

'Then I will stay for a few more hours. In the meantime, I will help clean the house,' he said as a plan started developing in his head.

Bells rang out throughout the village later that afternoon. The villagers immediately stopped what they were doing and began to make their way to the church. Father Yionnis and the junior priests were running up the aisles of the church making sure the flower arrangements were in place. The six open coffins of the executed men were lined up. A group of Turkish Soldiers stood outside the church guarding the entrance, while more patrolled the roads leading to it. The first of the mourners arrived and the soldiers pointed for them to walk into the Church. Father Yionnis greeted them and escorted them to their seats. The first two rows were reserved for the families of the executed men. A small trickle of people soon turned into a full flow. The Father peered outside, and the queue stretched all the way down the road. Within a few minutes the church was packed to the rafters. The grieving families spoke to the priest and the decision was taken to close the coffins as it became too distressing to see the mutilated bodies. The Turkish Captain stood outside giving orders to the other soldiers but was distracted when he saw Giovanni and Deraia walking at snail's pace towards the church. Giovanni holding on to her as her eighty-year-old legs took small step after small step. The Captain told the soldiers to clear the path for them to enter the church and as they walked past, the Captain nodded at Giovanni who returned the acknowledgement. Giovanni and Dareia had to stand by the doorway and with so many people in front of them it was impossible to see the Priest and the coffins. Father Yionnis' voice was barely audible drowned out by the crying and sobbing.

'I will leave you here I am going to help carry one of the coffins,' Giovanni informed Dareia as he pushed through the crowd of mourners.

'These men were fathers, sons, brothers, and to lose them in this act of brutality is a way I cannot understand, it is an act only our lord can make sense of,' Father Yionnis emotionally shouted out.

Outside the Turkish troops moved back so they were beyond the confines of the church grounds. The mourners started to slowly exit the church and to the yard where the gravediggers were desperately trying to finish digging the last of the six graves. The crowd then parted as Father Yionnis solemnly walked out carrying a large wooden cross followed by his two junior priests and behind them came the line of coffins, each coffin being carried by six pallbearers. Giovanni was carrying the last coffin that of Bedros. The Turkish Captain whispered into the ear of the interpreter who walked over to Father Yionnis who was standing in front of the graves.

'The Captain said that you need to bury them quickly, a quick blessing each and start the burials,' the interpreter told him.

'Please, we must respect the families of the dead men,' the Father said angrily.

'I am just passing on the order,' the interpreter said sternly before walking off.

'Can the pallbearers please place the coffins straight into the graves,' the Father announced.

One by one the wooden coffins were placed into the graves. Giovanni helped lower Bedros into the grave and then walked over to speak to Father Yionnis. The Turkish Captain looked on impatiently, wanting to leave the village as soon as possible.

Father Yionnis said a blessing and prayer for each of the deceased before the grave diggers started covering the coffins. A few of the mourners began to leave the church yard and the Father gestured to everyone to leave, and en masse everyone filed out. Turkish soldiers stood on the other side of the road. The widow of Bedros walked across the road and stood in front of the Captain.

'Murderer,' she shouted before spitting in his face.

The Captain smiled but stood still, this acted as a catalyst and more of the mourners came across the road shouting abuse at the Turks. A couple of the soldiers moved forward but the Captain ordered them to fall back in line.

'BANG!' a shot rang out and panic ensued, the mourners ran away from the church while the soldiers were unsure where the shot had come from. The crowd cleared and laying in the road was the Turkish Captain, other soldiers attended to him, but blood poured from the wound in the middle of his chest. The first Lieutenant tried to stem the flow of blood, but he could not find a pulse and realised that the Captain had died and that he was now the highest-ranking officer of the regiment. By now the crowd had completely dispersed and only Father Yionnis stood at the front of the church. The Lieutenant grabbed the interpreter by his sleeve and spoke to him and rushed over to the priest.

'Did you see who fired the shot?' the interpreter asked Father Yionnis.

The Father shook his head. The Lieutenant drew his sword intent on using it, Father Yionnis closed his eyes but looking round he could see the other soldiers watching him. If the Captain had been in his position he would have probably killed the Father, but he asked himself if this kind of retribution was necessary, especially when it was evident that the Father had not shot the Captain. He put his sword away and walked back and stood over the body of the Captain.

'Wrap his body, we are leaving,' The Lieutenant shouted out.

The other soldiers were left perplexed by his decision and one of the other officers approached him.

'Are we not going to find the person who shot the Captain?' The officer asked.

'We have spent too long in this village, and they have already paid the price,' the Lieutenant said pointing in the direction of the graves.

The Captain's body was wrapped in two cloths and placed in a cart and a ceremonial flag placed on top. The whole regiment was lined up outside the Church and the Lieutenant mounted on his horse raised his hand and this was the signal for the regiment to move in unison. The cavalry led the way followed by the infantry, and bringing up the rear, the carts carrying the ammunitions and other supplies. The final cart contained the body of the Captain.

As the dust settled Father Yionnis entered the church and walked to the back. Hidden behind one of the pillars was an opening that led into the Father's room. Seated there was Giovanni with a pistol on the table.

'They have left,' the Father informed him.

'I must leave as well.'

'Giovanni, I urge you to stay, this village needs you,' pleaded the Father.

'I need to be near my family.'

'Go and get them from Famagusta and bring them back. If you keep a low profile the Turks will be tolerable. Yes, we will live under their laws and pay them taxes but we will still be able to live our day to day lives. I will still serve God through this church. My family is the village and you; you are my family. If you leave Cyprus you will probably never return, if you decide to stand up against the Turks and fight them you will die,' the Father said as he sat next him. Giovanni shook his head.

'My family have led a privileged life on this Island and what has frightened them is this life is coming to an end. So, we either we flee or fight,' Giovanni explained.

'But you are a Cypriot. Will you be happy if you go and live in Venice?' The Father asked.

'If my wife and children are content then I am content.'

Father Yionnis looked at Giovanni not convinced that he was wholly truthful in his answer.

'I have to go and organize the head stones for the graves,' the Father said and promptly left the room. Giovanni, picking up his pistol, followed him and left the church and hastily walked to his house.

Father Yionnis' words rang around Giovanni's head, he was a Cypriot and killing the Turkish Captain imbued a sense of satisfaction, satisfaction of fighting to protect his land. The pressing matter therefore for him was to journey to Nicosia and help his father, uncle and brothers defend the City. Avoiding the Turkish regiments on his way to Nicosia would prove a challenge, but he decided to travel through the forest and mountains. The mountain paths were treacherous, but the advantage would be he would not come across any Turkish soldiers. He took one last walk through the olive groves before he rode off through the fields and up the hill. On the other side of the village Turkish Soldiers appeared followed by a horse drawn carriage with a large cannon attached at the back. The Turkish Lieutenant stood next to the canon as the gunners placed the canon in position and he pointed towards the church.

'Destroy the church,' ordered the Lieutenant.

Gunpowder was poured down the bore of the barrel before the cannon ball placed down the bore.

'Light the fuse when you are ready,' instructed the Lieutenant.

'Get back!' shouted the gunner.

He lit the torch paper, and everyone stood back and covered their ears. The sound of the exploding cannon ripped through the village and adjoining landscape. The cannon ball missed the church landing just infront on the road. Father Yionnis and his two assistants ran out. The Turkish gunner raised the barrel of the cannon a few inches before the gunpowder and cannon ball were packed in and fired. Father Yionnis and the two junior priests ran for the cover of the trees on the other side of the road. The church sustained a direct hit destroying the front façade. In the distance Giovanni heard the sound of the cannon and stopped, and turned to look in the direction of the village, and he heard another explosion. He waited for a few moments before continuing to Nicosia. The Turkish troops attached the cannon to the back of the carriage and the Lieutenant raised his arm to signify withdrawal. Father Yionnis stared at the ruins of the Church, tears rolling down his red cheeks. He fell to his knees, clasped his hands and looked up to heaven.

SIX

Terra, 1775

Water gushed from the well and Abdullah Cavus threw his hands up in the air in celebration.

'Seal it,' he shouted to two of his workers.

He looked out surveying all his land, from the banks of the dried-out stream to the ancient olive groves that stretched as far as the eye could see. Water from the old Venetian well would bring a new lease of life to the trees and make Terra one of the most attractive villages in that region of the Island. Abdullah distributed the water to the fields, and this revitalized the olive trees, but the problem he had was that he did not have enough workers to pick the olives as there were only a handful of families who lived in the village. Abdullah had arrived in Terra the previous year. The village had been uninhabited for over two hundred years and Abdullah had discovered the village when he lived in Lefke. After thirty years as a soldier in the Janissary corps he found the transformation to civilian life tough especially abandoning the strict disciplined life of a Janissary to a more idyllic lifestyle, but this soon changed when he married his wife Bahar and started a family. He saw the potential to develop Terra and insure his family's future. Soon discovery of the water spread like wildfire and a message came to Abdullah that the Muhassil, the Sultan's senior tax collector on the Island, wanted to visit Terra.

It was the height of summer and some of Abdullah's children were playing in the fields, he had seven children ranging from sixteen down to four years old. His oldest son, Serif, helped him in the fields, it was back breaking work. but his dream was to grow Terra into a thriving village and this day would go a long way in fulfilling his dream. Abdullah was dressed in his old Janissary uniform and tucked his gold handled dagger into a prominent position in his belt. Bahar wore a long white silk dress and even his children were in their fineries. Serif ran into the bedroom.

'He is here!' he exclaimed.

Two men on horse back arrived outside Abdullah's house followed by a horse drawn carriage. The coachman jumped down from the carriage and opened the door and the Muhassil stepped down. Abdullah and his family stood in a line. Abdullah stared at the Muhassil recognizing him from a previous encounter and approached him.

'You must be Abdullah Cavus,' the Muhassil asked him, and Abdullah bowed his head in acknowledgement.

'I am Sadik Pasha. I have come to see this well you have found. Can you take me to see it?' requested Sadik.

'I will take you immediately, Pasha.'

Abdullah led Sadik along the path towards the well.

'Your face looks very familiar to me,' Sadik informed Abdullah.

'Before my retirement I was a Sergeant in the Janissary corps in Lefkosa, so maybe you saw me there. Ahmet Corbaci, the Commander of the Janissaries is a close friend of mine, we served together,' Abdullah replied.

'Ahmet Corbaci, I know him well, yes, I tend to keep out of his way,' Sadik said. 'Why did you move here?'

'I lived in Lefke for sixteen years but as the family expanded the house became too small to accommodate me, my wife and my seven children,' Abdullah replied.

'Seven children,' said the surprised Sadik, 'you have one more than me.'

'I wanted a big enough house and some land to cultivate, and someone mentioned this village called Terra and here we are.'

The pair approached the well and Abdullah turned on the tap and the water gushed out. Sadik cupped his hand and drank the water.

'The water is cold and tastes so sweet, where does this water come from?' he asked.

'The Venetians started digging the well diverting water from the stream, but they did not complete it when they abandoned the village,' Abdullah explained.

'And this is all your land?' Sadik asked pointing in the direction of the olive trees.

'Yes, but I have no workers to help me. Houses have been built but they have no inhabitants,' Abdullah explained.

'Show me the rest of the village.'

Abdullah and Sadik walked side by side and they came across some ruins soon after.

'Was there are building here?' asked Sadik pointing at the stones.

'A church stood here during the times of the Venetians; this was a Greek village, but it was abandoned during the Turkish invasion. We found remains of many buildings. You can see the land is fertile and there used to be a stream running through the village and they grew olives in the land next to the stream. The name Terra is derived from the Latin word terra firma meaning firm land, it was probably so named during the Roman or Byzantine times,' he explained to a fascinated Sadik.

'Producing olive oil can make you a wealthy man. I can see the problem if you had no water and no labour but you have water now, so now you need workers,' Sadik observed. The men meandered down the old village road until they reached the olive groves and then onto Abdullah's house. The pair sat down outside in the shade. One of Abdullah's daughters, Deniz, bought out a jug of water and bread, olives, and cheese.

'That walk was thirsty work.' Sadik said as he gulped down the jug of water.

'Deniz, can you bring more water,' asked Abdullah.

'Your daughter is very pretty,' Sadik said quietly.

'Yes, she turned sixteen a few days ago.'

'I want to help you and I want to see this village prosper because it has a lot of potential. There is something I can do to increase the number of people who live here. All villages must pay tax but if I classify Terra as a farm then you and all inhabitants will be exempt from paying tax. I will sign a decree stating that Terra is a farm. I will guarantee this will see an influx of new blood come to the village,' proclaimed Sadik.

'Thank you, Pasha,' Abdullah said bowing his head.

'I will sign this decree immediately when I get back to Lefkosa. So, go to all the neighbouring villages. I will visit the village three months from this day and see what effect the decree has had,' the Pasha informed Abdullah as he stood up and walked towards his carriage. Abdullah took the Sadik's hand and kissed the back of it and then placed it on his forehead.

'I thank you again.'

Sadik climbed into the carriage and gave one last stare to Deniz, who stood behind her Father.

'I will see you in three months,' Sadik Pasha said as his carriage pulled away.

News spread fast of Terra's exemption from tax and dozens of families soon arrived. Abdullah sold parts of his land to the new arrivals and helped them build houses. He invested the money from the sale of his land into buying machinery, including an olive presser that he had to bring all the way from Paphos. He employed ten workers to maintain and harvest the olives. Water from the well was directed to the olive groves through an elaborate system of pipes, and whether it was due to the water or the fertilizer Abdullah used, but the trees produced the largest olives anyone had ever seen, and due to the size, the olives produced copious amounts of oil. Abdullah increased his fleet of carts and purchased huge metal vats to store the oil. Demand soon increased and to keep up with the orders Abdullah doubled his workforce. His olive oil was sold in Polis, in Paphos, and he even delivered to Lefkosa. One day Abdullah received a message that Sadik Pasha had invited him to his mansion in Lefkosa. Abdullah hired a grand carriage to take him to Lefkosa. Following the carriage was a cart containing large vases of olive oil that he would present to Pasha as a gift. The Pasha's residence in Nicosia, the Saray, was the old Palazzo del Governo built in the Venetian times. Abdullah was escorted through the house and into the lush garden. Sat at a table in the middle of a carefully manicured lawn was Sadik Pasha.

'Abdullah Cavus join me for some refreshments,' Sadik said beckoning him over. Abdullah stood.

'No, no need for such formalities sit down and help yourself,' Sadik said with a mouthful of sweet cake.

'I hear Terra has become a very prosperous village under your stewardship and what can I say about the olive oil you produce.'

'It has Pasha, and as a gift of gratitude, I have brought you a large supply of my olive oil.'

'I thank you,' Sadik said.

'No, I must thank you,' interrupted Abdullah. 'If it were not for your help I would not be here today.'

'Yes, I admit you have prospered enormously from my generosity and I do not begrudge you one little bit, but there is something you could possibly help me with,' Sadik said.

'Yes, of course Pasha, however I can help, I will.'

'It must be evident to you that I am getting old, retirement is around the corner. So, I need to be invigorated, something to keep me youthful such as a new wife,' Sadik said.

Abdullah gave him a puzzled stare.

Sadik continued, 'There are lots and lots of beautiful women on this Island, but the only one I think of day in, and day out is your beautiful daughter.'

It soon became clear what the Pasha wanted.

'Are you talking about my daughter, Deniz?' Abdullah asked seeking clarity.

'Yes, the very one,' Sadik said bouncing up and down on his chair. 'Tell me the truth Abdullah, is she married or promised to another man?' the excited Pasha asked.

'No.'

'That is the best news I have heard for a very long time. So, Abdullah, I would like to take your daughter as my wife. Do not concern yourself with any of the arrangements I will have everything taken care of.'

Abdullah was in a state of shock.

'Pasha, I do not know what to say. All my family admire you, but my daughter is not ready for marriage yet. If you are willing to wait a couple more years then she would think about it,' Abdullah said trying to gloss over the situation.

'Abdullah, you do not seem to understand. I am not asking for your daughter in marriage, for everything I have done for you and the prosperity I have bought you and all the inhabitants of your village. I am just demanding my dues,' Sadik calmly said.

'Pasha, just to clarify, you want my daughter as a payment for helping me?' a red-faced Abdullah said in an increased tone of voice.

'Abdullah, I would not word it in such a way, it is not a payment but you just returning the favour.'

Abdullah seething at what had just heard stared at Sadik and suddenly stood up.

'Sadik Pasha, thank you for inviting me to your home, but I must go, it is a long journey home.'

'Are you ignoring me?' Sadik questioned in a raised voice.

'I must decline your proposal Pasha, I am grateful for all your assistance, and please accept my gift, but our relationship must end now.'

Sadik slammed the palm of his hand on the table. Abdullah stood back, standing as in preparing for a duel.

'I am a reasonable man. So, I will give you time to think about my proposal. One week today I will travel to Terra expecting good news from you. If I do not receive that good news, there will be consequences. I will tear up the decree I signed giving a tax exemption to all inhabitants, and I will demand that tax backdated from the day I signed the decree is paid by all the villagers,' at this point Sadik laughed. 'Yes, since the village is enjoying such wealth, I will double the tax.'

Abdullah just stared at him showing no emotion, he then turned and walked away.

'I will see you in a week Abdullah,' Sadik shouted out.

The journey back to Terra was probably the worst of Abdullah's life, as a million and one thoughts passed through his mind. The idea of his daughter marrying a Pasha, marrying into wealth and into the Turkish elite should have made him proud, but there was something that repulsed him. Maybe the fact that the Pasha was even older than himself or the way the Pasha spoke about her as an object he could demand at will. In retrospect Abdullah, a principled and honourable man, saw this act as disrespectful, especially from a high ranking official, a man chosen by the Sultan. His family were waiting for him anticipating good news, but when he arrived it was evident by the look on his face that the outcome had been the reverse. Bahar took Abdullah by the arm and sat him down as he remained silent.

'The Pasha will tear up the decree and start demanding tax from everyone in the village, if I do not agree to his proposal, indeed he will double the tax for all inhabitants of Terra,' explained Abdullah looking painful.

'What is his proposal? Bahar asked.

'Not a proposal but a demand, he demands that Deniz be his wife,' he said turning his head to Deniz.

'But father, I thought you would be pleased that the Pasha would want my hand in marriage. It will give our family security for the rest of our lives and the lives of my children and all your grandchildren,' Deniz said seemingly open to the idea.

'Yes, Abdullah, this is good news, the Pasha wants to marry our daughter. We should be shouting it from the rooftops,' Bahar said echoing Deniz's sentiments.

Abdullah sat back in his chair surprised by the reaction of his wife and daughter.

'You must say yes to him,' urged Bahar.

'I will marry him,' Deniz said skipping out the room and singing 'I am marrying the Pasha.'

Bahar clasped Abdullah's hands.

'When will you tell the Pasha that Deniz will accept his marriage proposal? She asked.

'In one week, he is coming here for an answer.'

'Yes, Yes, Yes, that is the answer. We must prepare for his visit, the whole village must know and there will be a grand turnout,' shouted out Bahar with excitement oozing out of her has she left the room going in search of Deniz leaving Abdullah in a state of confusion. He asked himself what had just happened and what was he to do now that Deniz wanted to marry the Pasha and that Bahar was in favour of it as well? His head told him that Deniz marrying the Pasha would mean his family would become one of the most powerful and wealthiest on the Island, but his heart still felt heavy in the sense of something did not feel right about it. The next day Abdullah wrote a letter to Ahmet Corbaci, Abdullah had been well educated, born to a military family he was sent to Istanbul at the age of thirteen to train as a Janissary and during the six years of training as well as learning the military aspects of an army recruit, he learnt to read and write in Arabic. He sealed the letter with the seal of the Janissaries and summoned Serif.

'I want you to take this letter to Lefkosa,' Serif stood in excitement. 'Go to the Janissaries' barracks and ask for Ahmet Corbaci, tell them you are my son, but insist you hand the letter to Corbaci, do not give it to anyone else.'

One week passed in a blink of an eye and one of the boys from the village who had been made a look out ran through the village.

'The Pasha is here; the Pasha is here!' shouted the boy at the top his squeaky voice, still a year or so away from his voice breaking.

He sprinted all the way to Abdullah's house and in through the house and out the back, where a lavish feast had been laid on. Tables of food were laid across the garden area.

'Bahar Teyze, the Pasha has arrived,' the boy slowly said completely out of breath. Bahar gave him a handful of cakes and the boy hid behind a tree and started to devour them.

From the house stepped out Deniz, her hair long and flowing and wearing a blue dress, that had been bought at the most fashionable clothing shop in Lefkosa. Baher ran up to her.

'You look so beautiful.'

'Thank you, mother, but where is father?'

As they looked around the garden out strode Abdullah, resplendent in his Janissary uniform, his left hand poised on the handle of his gold dagger.

'Deniz, you look amazing,' he said with a huge beaming smile.

'Thank you, father, so do you.'

Sadik Pasha arrived dressed traditionally, he wore a gold inner robe with long sleeves, a short kaftan made of gold silk, and a light long blue outer robe. Stepping out from his covered carriage the heat had taken its toll and sweat patches were clearly visible on the Pasha's clothes. He was flanked by two burley mustachioed guards, both carrying large jagged edged daggers. Abdullah greeted him by kissing the back of his hand before placing it on his forehead.

'Welcome Pasha, follow me,' Abdullah ushered the Pasha around the side of the house to the garden and there Sadik got a brief glimpse of Deniz before Bahar escorted her inside.

'Pasha, this is your table please be seated, your guards can sit by that table,' Abdullah said pointing to a table nearer the house. Abdullah sat opposite Sadik.

'I must commend you on your hospitality Abdullah Cavus, I was not expecting this kind of welcome, a much pleasant surprise. A week has passed since my proposal and I have been wondering what your decision would be.' Sadik was cut off in mid flow as one of Abdullah's other daughters Meli, placed a plate of freshly baked olive bread in front of Sadik.

'Please try it, the olives in the bread are from my trees.'

Sadik broke a portion of the bread and ate it.

'It is still warm.'

'My wife baked it this morning.'

'Back to my proposal,' Sadik said raising his hands.

'Pasha you can have my daughter's hand in marriage,' said Abdullah.

'Wonderful, long may the prosperity of you, your family and the village of Terra continue,' Sadik exclaimed.

'Meli, can you go inside and ask Deniz to come out?' Meli nodded at her Father's instruction and hurried inside.

'Pasha, so by my understanding all inhabitants of the village would still be exempt for paying any tax?' Abdullah asked.

'Yes, I am a man of my word,' Sadik said before being distracted by the sight of Deniz coming out of the house. Sadik stood up as Deniz and Bahar approached him. Sadik took Deniz's hand and kissed it.

'You are most beautiful, I have asked your father for your hand in marriage, and he has accepted, but being a modern man, I would like to ask you for your acceptance,' Sadik asked Deniz, who glanced at her father.

'Pasha, it is an honour to be asked for my hand in marriage from you and I accept your proposal,' Deniz said.

This brought an immense smile onto Sadik's face.

'Please, all sit down. We must discuss arrangements,' Sadik eagerly said.

'The wedding day will be one week from today in Lefkosa. I have spoken to the Imam and he will conduct the religious ceremony at the mosque before we move to my residence for the reception.'

'Why so soon, Pasha?' Abdullah asked.

'Why wait any longer? I am sure Deniz would like to be a Pasha's wife as soon as possible. I am not mistaken in my view and I am sure Deniz will agree with that,' Sadik said looking at Deniz.

After a pause, Deniz nodded her head.

'One week is long enough to prepare for a wedding,' she said.

Sadik threw his hand in the air in jubilation, but the joy was not reciprocated by Abdullah.

'This wedding will be best this Island has ever seen,' boasted Sadik.

'My family would also like some form of wedding ceremony held here in the village,' Bahar requested.

'This is my intention, I would not be disrespectful to your family or the village. We can hold a ceremony here in Terra in two weeks from today so a week after our marriage in Lefkosa. Would you all be amenable with that date?' Sadik asked.

Abdullah looked at Bahar and Deniz before nodding his head in acceptance. Sadik took out a bag of coins.

'Take it,' he said to Abdullah reaching out the bag of coins, 'use this to make arrangements for the wedding here in two weeks, my donation. All the preparations for the ceremony next week are all in hand.'

'Thank you, Pasha for your donation,' Abdullah reluctantly said.

'Please, could you grant me permission to speak to Deniz on my own?' asked Sadik.

Abdullah raised his hand to gesture his approval and Sadik stood up and offered his hand to Deniz, who reached out and held it.

'Shall we go for a little walk?' Sadik asked Deniz and she nodded.

They walked off together and Bahar stared at Abdullah who in turn was staring at Sadik and his daughter.

'What is wrong with you? Our daughter is going to marry the Pasha and you are still unhappy. I cannot understand that someone like you, someone steeped in Turkish tradition would object to this,' said a cross Bahar.

'I want the best for all my children, and yes Deniz will marry into the elite of Turkish society. I do not deny that, but my reservation is the way he forced me into agreeing to the marriage. Forgiveness is not in my nature,' he said in a cold-hearted way.

Sadik and Deniz walked down the avenue of olive trees and she held on to him as he stumbled, and this seemed to highlight their forty-year age gap. Abdullah strolled over to them.

'My dear Pasha, are you hurt? I saw you fall.'

'No, I did not fall, it was a mere stumble. Fortunately, Deniz was by my side and helped me.'

'It appears to me that you require a nurse rather than a wife,' Abdullah sarcastically remarked.

'I thank Allah for finding me your beautiful daughter,' said Sadik looking up to the sky.

'In the end Allah looks after all of us,' came Abdullah's sharp reply.

Once Deniz and Bahar went back inside the house Sadik gestured to Abdullah to come over.

'My friend, you have made the right decision and while I am Pasha you will enjoy great privileges. I want you to supply the Governor's residence with olive oil for the next year. You will receive the market price,' said Sadik

'I thank you for your kind gesture. Supplying the Governor's residence would be a great honour, but not to show disrespect, could you recommend me to all your family and friends. You know I produce the best quality olive oil on the Island and spreading the word would enhance my reputation. I am certain making your perspective Father-in-Law happy would be one of your priorities.'

The remark made Sadik laugh.

'Yes, you will be my Father-in-law. That is very funny,' chuckled Saidk. 'Why not ask Ahmet Corbaci if you can supply the Janissary barracks with their olive oil? I am sure they go through gallons of oil.'

'Yes, Pasha. Thank you for your thoughts. I have written to Ahmet Corbaci and I hope to meet him in the next week or so,' confirmed Abdullah.

That last comment made Sadik's face change to an uncomfortable look.

'You have written to Ahmet Corbaci? About supplying him with olive oil,' asked Sadik.

'Yes, one of many things in my letter. You know we are good friends, so I wrote about all kinds of matters.'

'Did you include in your letter that I am to marry your daughter?'

'I think I may have mentioned it in a sentence or two,' came Abdullah's vague answer.

'Anyway, I must go before it gets too late. So, a week today my carriages will arrive early in the morning and bring you, Deniz and your family to Lefkosa. Leave the rest with me. All you have to do is bring Deniz and of course yourself.'

'Pasha, it will the proudest day of my, and my family's life,' remarked Abdullah.

Sadik and his two guards climbed into the carriage and departed the village.

Seven days passed with ease. If Abdullah had the power to slow down time or even stop time, he would have surely used it. Abdullah had been unable to sleep and spent the night wandering around the fields and therefore consequentially had left him with red bleary eyes. He had come to terms with the marriage of his daughter to the Pasha and his main concern now was that the wedding would run without problems. A splash or two of cold water on his face made him feel more awake. Deniz and her three sisters had changed into their dresses whilst Bahar was combing their hair. Serif and his two brothers dressed in identical outfits, like Abdullah's Janissary uniform. There was a knock at the door and Abdullah opened it to find the Pasha's carriage drivers standing there.

'Abdullah Cavus, your carriages await you,' one of the carriage drivers said.

'We will be with you soon. The carriages are here,' Abdullah shouted out.

Abdullah escorted Deniz onto the first carriage and he, Bahar and Serif joined her. His other five children went in the second carriage. The journey to Lefkosa started well with the early morning mountain breezes making it quite bearable, but once the late summer heat set in the carriages became conductors of heat. Abdullah's back became soaked in sweat, becoming very uncomfortable for him. It was just after midday that the outskirts of Lefkosa came into sight.

'We are here,' said Bahar as she held Deniz's hand.

The carriages passed by the old city walls built by the Venetians and into the city passing by Turkish built buildings such as the Yeni Han before coming to a halt outside the Pasha's residence. They were greeted by servants who provided cold refreshing drinks before being escorted to the bathrooms. Abdullah heard music and followed the sound to the magnificent garden where he found the source of the music - a ten-piece military band and standing in the middle of the garden was Sadik Pasha, his golden turban glistening in the sun. He was ordering around his staff making certain that all the tables were lavishly decorated and covered with a fabric canopy that provided shade from the intense sun. An army of servants started to bring out chairs and soon after large plates of food began appearing and being put on the tables. Sadik noticed Abdullah and walked up to him and embraced him.

'Abdullah, your table is ready,' he said pointing towards it. 'I am waiting for the Imam to arrive. Where is Deniz?'

'The journey from Terra was long and hot, so my wife and daughters are refreshing themselves.'

'Guests are beginning to arrive, come with me and we can greet them together,' Sadik said guiding Abdullah to the entrance of the garden, which was accessible through the side of the house. A sudden influx of people descended, Sadik and Abdullah greeted everyone of the guests, amongst the arrivals was the Imam, and he took Abdullah to one side.

'Allah blesses you, your daughter and all your family. You are a retired janissary so you will understand the connection between Islamic laws and the laws of the Turkish administration. At times, the Pasha fails to understand the adherence of Allah's teachings and I must guide him so I hope that you could assist with guiding him,' the Imam requested of Abdullah, who seemed completely disinterested in the Imam's words.

'I will become the Father-in-law of the Pasha, so I would assume he would court my advice,' said Abdullah.

'May god be with you,' said the Imam as he held Abdullah's hand.

The Imam then spoke to Sadik about the timings of the ceremony as Abdullah wandered off to look for his family, but in the corner of his eye he saw a recognizable flash of colour. Turning his head, he recognized the Janissary uniform and the man in it, Ahmet Corbaci, commander of the Janissary regiment in Lefkosa and Abdullah's old friend.

'Ahmet! Ahmet!' shouted Abdullah.

Ahmet heard his name being called and it took a few moments to pinpoint the direction of the person and a big wide grin greeted the oncoming Abdullah, the pair embraced.

'Abdullah my brother, how are you?' asked Ahmet.

Ahmet was an imposing figure with a long beard with the strands of grey protruding out.

'I feel so happy to see you Ahmet, or do I have to call you Ahmet Corbaci?'

'No, you can call me your brother,' he clarified with a smile.

'Did you receive my letter Ahmet?'

'I did, that is why I am here. You must feel like the proudest father in the World, you daughter marrying a Pasha,' presumed Ahmet.

'I am,' Abdullah said unconvincingly.

'When are you holding a ceremony in Terra, tomorrow or the next day?' Ahmet asked.

'A week from today.'

Ahmet stared at him confusingly.

'But it can not be. The Pasha would have left the Island by then,' Ahmet informed him.

'I do not understand why would he leave the Island?'

'Has he not informed you? His tenure as Muhsasil, finishes today. A new Muhassil arrives tomorrow. I received the letter from the Sultan one month ago. The letter also confirms that Sadik Pasha is being sent to Jerusalem,' Ahmet confirmed.

'What will happen to Deniz?' asked Abdullah.

'The wife of a Muhassil will follow him to wherever he is assigned. He will be leaving on a ship from Famagusta to Sidon in three days, so there will be no wedding in Terra.'

'He has been dishonest to me. He passed a decree that all inhabitants of Terra would pay no taxes but then issued me an ultimatum that if I did not accept his proposal of marriage to Deniz, he would rescind the tax decree.'

'All decrees would be reviewed by the new Muhassil. From midnight tonight Sadik Pasha has no authority on the Island,' Ahmet said.

'I cannot let Deniz go to Jerusalem. If she goes with him, I will probably never see her again.'

Ahmet nodded his head in agreement.

'I must agree that he has been dishonest with you. His behaviour is not the way one of the Sultan's officials should behave. Abdullah it is not too late. I will support you in whatever decision you come to,' Ahmet reassured him.

Abdullah looked around the garden to see Sadik laughing in conversation with one of the guests, Deniz and Bahar were standing close by Sadik with the rest of his children. He was torn. Deniz was enjoying the happiest day of her life, but in his eyes, she was marrying a dishonest cheat and for Abdullah they could only be one outcome. He gestured at Ahmet who gave a slight nod of his head to signify that he understood Abdullah's decision. He marched towards Sadik with Ahmet in tow and interrupted him in mid flow of a conversation with a guest.

'Pasha, I must talk to you urgently,' Abdullah said in a raised voice, loud enough for most of the people in the garden to hear.

'What is wrong?' uttered Sadik.

'You know my friend, Ahmet Corbaci,' Abdullah said as Ahmet gave Sadik a menacing stare.

'Yes.'

'He has enlightened me with some disturbing news and I would like you to clarify this. If you are leaving Cyprus in three days, how could you and Deniz attend your wedding ceremony in Terra a week today, when you will be in Jerusalem? Did I misunderstand you when you said the wedding would be in Terra? did you mean Jerusalem?

Deniz, Bahar and most of the other guests gathered round listening intently. Sadik was lost for words.

'Dishonest, that is the only word to describe you. After today's wedding you would have forced Deniz to come with you to Jerusalem and we would host a wedding ceremony in Terra with no bride or groom attending. I have decided there will be no wedding today, tomorrow, or next week. Bahar and Deniz gather the children we are heading back to Terra.'

'Go, go back to your rat-infested village. I will pass one final decree to triple the taxes paid by all inhabitants of the village.' Shouted Sadik. Upon hearing this Abdullah made a beeline for Sadik but was stopped by Ahmet.

'Go home Abdullah. I will deal with this,' said Ahmet.

Abdullah waited for Bahar, Deniz and other children before heading out the garden.

'I will ruin you Abdullah Cavuz,' shouted Sadik.

'No, you will not,' said Ahmet as he took a hold of Sadik's collars and pulled him forward. 'You have no more authority on this Island. You will stay in your room until it is time for you to leave. There will be no more decrees, no more laws until the new Muhassil arrives.' Ahmet said letting go of his collars.

'What authority do you have?' questioned Sadik.

'Let me explain, firstly, all the soldiers in this building, in this city, and on this Island listen to me. Secondly, I have the power to try any person who I believe has committed treason against the Sultan. The penalty for treason is death. So, Sadik Pasha I would go to your room until it is time to leave the Island.'

Sadik looked at his guards but they all looked away. With all eyes on him he had no alternative but to walk into the house. Outside, Abdullah asked the carriage drivers to take them back to Terra, but the men told him that they only answered to the Pasha. At that point Ahmet came marching out.

'You two take Abdullah Cavus and his family back to their village,' he barked at them which made them run to the carriages and helped the family on.

'Abdullah do not worry there will not be any repercussions I will handle the safe passage of the Pasha out of Cyprus. I would like to visit Terra soon.'

'Come soon Ahmet. Thank you for today.'

'There is no need to thank me. I was just helping my brother janissary,' said Ahmet.

The journey back to Terra was silent. Deniz was in tears for most of the journey, but Abdullah could not be sure if this were due to grief over the dishonesty of Sadik Pasha or the fact that her chance to marry a wealthy Pasha had evaporated or maybe a bit of both. In a way Abdullah regrated the whole situation of meeting Sadik Pasha and accepting his proposal to increase the prosperity of himself and the village, but that was history, Sadik was no more, and Abdullah was now focused on the future.

Water flowed from the pipe giving the olive trees the sustenance they required to fulfil their optimum growth potential. These olives were becoming plump and full of oil and having received a letter from Ahmet Corbaci agreeing for Abdullah to supply the Janissary garrison in Lefkosa with olive oil, the requirement was now to increase the production by two-fold. With a month left before the harvest it seemed that Abdullah would fulfil his production demands. Serif ran down from the house to find Abdullah who was at the far end of his fields.

'Father, Ahmet Corbaci has arrived to visit you and there is another man with him,' said an out of breath Serif.

'Who is this other man?' asked a concerned Abdullah.

'He did not introduce himself.'

Abdullah marched towards the house in the boots he wore in the fields whilst Serif struggled to keep pace with him. Ahmet Corbaci was sat outside the house with an unknown man while four Janissaries soldiers tendered to the six horses.

'Abdullah how are you my friend,' Ahmet shouted out as he jumped out of his seat and kissed and embraced Abdullah.

'Why did you not forewarn me of your visit. I have nothing prepared,' said Abdullah.

'We are just passing through and I wanted to see the olives that will produce all the oil and introduce you to the Island's new Muhassil. This is Es-Seyyid Omer.'

Abdullah shook hands with Omer.

'Pleasure to meet you. I do not know what Ahmet has told you, but I had an interesting relationship with your predecessor Sadik Pasha.'

'Ahmet has told me all about the situation with Sadik Pasha and that is the reason I wanted to come and meet and reassure you that I will fully endorse the decree signed by him giving all inhabitants of Terra a tax exemption and this will continue until my tenure ends.' confirmed Omer.

'I must thank you.' Abdullah quickly responded.

'And be rest assured I will not be asking you for your daughter's hand in marriage,' Omer said as all three men began to laugh.

SEVEN

Terra, 1957

The night air was punctured by the sound of a rattling engine of a motorcycle making its way through the winding roads of Terra before coming to a halt outside a house. Yilmaz Mehmet of the Cyprus Police Mobile Reserve took his goggles off and pushed his bike behind the fence at the front of the house so it could not be seen from the road. He crept behind the house and hearing a noise he stood still and put his hand on his pistol holster, but it turned out to be one of the village dogs wandering around looking for a new adventure. Yilmaz tried the back door and to his surprise it was unlocked, so he walked in searching each room before coming to a bedroom. He pushed the slightly open door until it fully opened and there asleep on the bed was a woman, Lutfiye, and next to her was a cot with a toddler fast asleep in it. He tiptoed to the bed and gave the woman a kiss on her forehead, this woke her up and her face lit up when she recognized her husband.

'What are doing here?' Lutfiye said in complete surprise.

'I have a few hours off before I return to the camp, so I thought I'll come a share the good news with you.'

'Let's go to the lounge before we wake Zorlu up,' Lutfiye whispered as she got out of bed and ushered him into the lounge.

'How is the boy?' he asked.

'He is still teething, and this is the first night he has gone to sleep at a decent hour. Come on tell me the good news?'

'I've been made Acting Sergeant,' he said to her with a big beaming smile.

'I thought you told me that they turned you down.'

'They refused to make me a Sergeant because I have not served five years, but my Inspector pushed them and the solution is to make me Acting Sergeant, I'll get the salary and privileges of a Sergeant, but I am not allowed to wear a Sergeant's stripes,' he explained.

'Amazing, when do you start?'

'With immediate effect was the exact words of the Inspector. We are on an operation tonight. We have had a tipoff that some terrorists are in hiding at Kykkos monastery, so I'm taking twenty men up there to search it,' Yilmaz said with a certain glee in his voice.

'But Troodos is an EOKA stronghold, it is dangerous, how many British soldiers have been killed up there?' she asked.

'Actually, a British patrol was ambushed two nights ago, the driver was killed, and the other three soldiers are in hospital in Polis.'

'That's what I mean. it's not safe,' she said concerned.

'What do you want me to do, it's the nature of my job.'

'How is the camp? What's it like sharing with the British soldiers?' 'We get on well with them, they are Fusiliers from a place called Lancashire, but they are building a separate camp for us,' Yilmaz said.

'Are you hungry? Your mum brought round a bean stew and rice, there's still some left in the pot on the stove.'

'No, I have to get back. Hopefully, I will hear about the house in Polis soon, once my papers come through, we can move, then we can be together every night.'

'Are they going to pay the rent for the house?' She questioned.

'Yes, they pay the full rent. Anyway, I must go,' and they hugged and kissed.

Yilmaz wheeled the motorcycle through the village, so the sound of the bike did not draw attention to himself and once he reached the outskirts, he started the engine and sped away into the pitch-black countryside. The army camp was just under nine miles away via the main road, but it was dangerous travelling on main roads due to the risk of terrorist attacks. There was an alternative route, but this road was an uneven dirt track that took longer, so Yilmaz decided to stay on the main road that went through Polis and onto the camp. Approaching Polis, he could see a light, ahead in the road, so he slowed down before coming to a halt. He took out his pistol and held on to it as he started accelerating until he reached the source of the light a small van parked on the side of the road. Yilmaz lowered his body and leaned to the other side of the bike as he went past the van. He looked back but could not see anyone, and after travelling a few hundred yards past, he stopped the bike and switched the engine off before dismounting and walking back towards the van, holding the pistol in his right hand. Voices appeared to be coming from the back of the van and Yilmaz walked behind, left hand ready to open the van door and right hand prepared to shoot. He opened the door to find a naked and startled man and woman in the back. They quickly grabbed their clothes and covered themselves.

'Your van lights are on. I would suggest if you wanted some privacy, you find somewhere more secluded and not by the side of the road. Where are both from?'

'Polis,' answered the man rather sheepishly.

'Put your clothes on and drive back to Polis,' ordered Yilmaz.

'Yes, we will,' the couple said in unison.

Yilmaz walked back to his bike smiling and shaking his head.

A couple of hours later a convoy left Limni army camp heading for Kyykos monastery. In front was a Land Rover carrying Yilmaz, Sergeant Ali and the driver Suleiman, followed by two trucks each carrying fourteen police mobile reservists. The Police Mobile Reserve was made up of entirely Turkish Cypriot policemen but under the command of the British army. Their primary role was to combat terrorist activities on the Island carried out by EOKA. The convoy headed into the forests of Troodos but they slowed down at an army roadblock. A soldier approached the Land Rover.

'Where are you going?' he asked.

'Kykkos monastery,' answered back Yilmaz.

'How many men are there in the two trucks?' the soldier asked.

'Thirty two men in total including the drivers and passengers,' replied Yilmaz.

The soldier waived them on

'This was the spot that a soldier was killed the other night,' Suleiman told the others.

'I just hope we are not being led into a trap at the monastery and this informant is reliable,' said a concerned Yilmaz.

'I was told that this informant in question has given us two tip-offs and, on both occasions, it led to several EOKA members being captured,' Ali shared with them.

'The only problem with these informants, is in the end they get found out and killed. I had an informant called Alexou and everything he told me was one hundred percent
accurate and one day he had information on the hideout of Grivas. We headed to this village prepared to capture him.

There was someone hidden at that house. Not Grivas, but the dead body of Alexou,' Yilmaz told them.
After a steep climb, the convoy reached the monastery and stopped a few hundred yards before the entrance.
'Take some of the men behind the monastery,' instructed Yilmaz.
The Police mobile reservists carried British army standard issue Sten submachine guns, effective at close quarter combat, and the men were all positioned as Yilmaz banged on the monastery door. An elderly monk opened the door.
'We are the police, and we are here to search the monastery,' Yilmaz said in Greek.
'Who are you searching for? Only monks live here,' the old monk said.
Yilmaz pushed the monk aside and the rest of the men rushed in.
'This is a holy building you have no right to enter,' the monk shouted at Yilmaz, who took out a piece of paper from his pocket and handed it to the monk.
'This is a police warrant and legally entitles us to search the monastery,' Yilmaz said as he briskly walked through the reception area and into the main courtyard.
'Round up all the monks and have them lined up in the courtyard. Search every room,' Yilmaz shouted.
All the monks in the monastery were ushered down into the courtyard. Some minutes later Sergeant Ali came running down to Yilmaz.
'We have searched all the rooms and there is no one here apart from these monks.'
'Can you all stand in a line,' Yilmaz shouted at the monks in Greek.
Some of the police men had to help shuffle some of the monks into a straight line. Yilmaz walked up to the start of

the line and began to walk down looking at each monk in the face. They were all elderly but half way down the line he stopped and starred intensely at one of the monks, his face looked far too young and taking one step forward Yilmaz yanked at the monks beard and it came off in his hand.

'Hands up!' shouted Yilmaz at the man as he drew his pistol. The man put his hand up and two of the policemen grabbed him and put handcuffs on him.

'Take him to one of the rooms,' Yilmaz ordered.

They pushed him into the nearest room and forcibly sat him into a chair.

'What's your name?' Yilmaz asked him but the man remained silent.

'Search him.'

They took off the man's robe to reveal a short sleeve shirt and trousers.

'Are you a member of EOKA?' Yilmaz asked him, but the man said nothing.

'I want a proper search of the monastery. I do not care if it takes all night. Keep him here and all the monks in one room.'

The search proved fruitless and with the terrorist in the back of one of the trucks they headed back to Polis.

The next day Yilmaz and some of the others were in the mess hall when Inspector Tapping, the Police unit commander, walked in and scanned the hall until he spotted Yilmaz.

'Acting Sergeant Yilmaz,' the Inspector said in a loud voice.

Yilmaz stood to attention.

'Sir,'

'Come with me,' ordered Tapping.

Yilmaz followed Tapping out of the hall while the others looked on while steam was still coming from his mug of tea.

'Chief Constable Robin is here, one of these unannounced visits, you know what I mean,' Tapping blurted out with Yilmaz completely oblivious to what he had just said. Chief Constable Robin, a second world war veteran, was talking to some of the other officers as Tapping and Yilmaz stood behind him. Robin turned to them.

'Chief Constable, this is Acting Sergeant Yilmaz, he led the unit that raided Kykkos monastery,' Tapping said at which point Yilmaz saluted Robin.

'I hear you captured one of those terrorists,' Robin said.

'Yes sir,' Yilmaz replied.

'You speak good English,' said Robin.

'He also speaks fluent Greek as well, Chief Constable,' interrupted Tapping.

'Tapping, I could do with a man like him, especially if he knows Greek. I want to visit some of the villages near here and the Acting Sergeant can be my interpreter. I also want to join the unit on patrol, see first-hand how the men operate.'

'We can certainly arrange that Chief Constable, Actually, we are setting up roadblocks outside Polis tonight,' Tapping informed him.

'Splendid, I look forward it. Acting Sergeant, I will see you tonight,' Robin and Yilmaz saluted each other.

'Tapping, where are the WCs around here?' asked Robin.

Yilmaz headed back to the mess hall and joined Sergeants Ali, Hasan and Ferdi.

'What did Tapping want? Ferdi asked.

'He introduced me to Chief Constable Robin and he's going to come on patrol with us tonight,' Yilmaz informed them. 'He also wants me to be his interpreter.'

'You seem to be the golden boy, Yilmaz. Two years you have been on the force and they have made you a Sergeant. It took me twenty years to become Sergeant. Are you giving the British special favours?' Ferdi said with a smirk.

With that Yilmaz banged on the table and stood up which forced Ferdi to stand up and the pair confronted each other.

'You're just a jealous bastard,' Yilmaz uttered in Ferdi's face.

Ali and Hasan stood and separated the pair.

'Come on, both of you need to cool off,' Hasan said pushing Yilmaz away. 'Let's go outside. Ignore Ferdi, he annoys everyone just like a mosquito,' said Hasan.

'They made him Sergeant because he has been on the force so long, nothing to do with ability,' said Yilmaz, his tone of voice still showing contempt for the man.

'Anyway, I have the day off tomorrow, is there anything you want from Terra?' Hasan asked.

'If you go past my mum's house see if she has made some borek.'

'Only if I can have a few of them,' Hasan said cheekily.

'When she sees you, I'm sure she will cook a fresh batch just for you.'

A land rover left the camp, Yilmaz was sat next to Suleiman and Chief Constable Robin and Inspector Tapping were sat in the back. Following was a truck of British soldiers all from the Lancashire Fusiliers. They drove to a point just outside Polis and stopped to set up the roadblock.

'How successful have these roadblocks been in terms of terrorists apprehended or weapons found?' Robin asked Tapping.

'To be honest Chief Constable, it's been pretty patchy. Last week two soldiers stopped a car and while they were searching it they found a cache of guns but before they confiscated the weapons the occupant of the car drove off,' Tapping explained.

'That is a case of bad training Tapping,' said Robin.

The roadblock was set up with the Land Rover and truck lights on full beam. A car approached and Yilmaz and two soldiers stood in the middle of the road and waved down the car, and Yilmaz approached it and told the driver in Greek to turn off the engine. Robin and Tapping walked closer so they could observe. Yilmaz took the keys out of the ignition and the soldiers began to search the car. Robin nudged Tapping and nodded his head in approval.

'That is how you conduct a search Tapping,' Robin quietly said.

After a couple more cars were searched the decision was taken to head back to camp. Robin and Tapping were required in the briefing room and they asked Yilmaz to come with them. Leading the briefing was Sergeant Mason.

'Gentlemen, we have just received news that Nikos Sampson has been captured,' Mason informed the others.

'Splendid news,' yelled Robin. 'How many soldiers has he killed?' he asked.

'At least fifteen Sir, but we think it may be higher,' Tapping replied.

'Hang the sod,' Robin mumbled.

'That is part of the news. We have received intelligence reports that a number of terrorists are hiding out in a village called Arodes,' Mason informed them.

'Arodes is where my wife is from,' interrupted Yilmaz.

'You must know the village then?' Tapping asked.

'Yes sir.'

Mason placed three sheets of paper on the table with the men's profiles on them.

'These are the three suspected terrorists and the homes of their families in the village.'

Robin examined the profiles.

'We must find them. These men have without doubt been involved in the recent killings in this area, so we must hunt them down. We plan to raid the village tomorrow; I rather fancy it myself. Sergeant Yilmaz can lead the reserves and we will bring a squad of fusiliers,' instructed Robin.

'Chief Constable, am I allowed to say something?' Yilmaz awkwardly asked.

'Of course, spit it out man,' said Robin.

'One problem, there is only one road from Polis to Arodes and if we drive there they will spot us a mile off,' Yilmaz said.

'How far is Arodes from Polis?' Robin asked.

'About eight miles,' Yilmaz replied.

'Eight miles, that's settled we will walk it. We hit the village in the middle of the night, that way no one sees or hears us,' insisted Robin as Tapping, Mason and Yilmaz all looked at each other with apprehension.

The following night the police unit and a unit from the Fusiliers set off on foot from Polis. Yilmaz was teamed up with Corporal Coles from the Fusiliers. Inspector Tapping and Chief Constable Robin followed closely behind. Yilmaz led the units through uneven paths and fields the men having to contend against rough undergrowth and the odd snake. Coles missed his footing on a downhill path and tumbled to the ground. Yilmaz rushed over and helped him up.

'Thank you,' Coles said trying to hide the embarrassment of his fall.

'Where in England are you from Corporal?' Yilmaz asked him.

'A town called Blackpool.'

'Do you miss it?'

'I miss my family, my friends, and I miss playing football,' Coles said.

'You play football. I play for my unit and we play against other police units throughout the Island,' Yilmaz explained.

'I used to play for Blackpool's youth team,' Coles revealed.

'Are Blackpool a good team?' Yilmaz asked having never heard of them.

'They were runners-up in the league to Manchester United last season.'

'Manchester United, I know of them. Do you play at the camp?'

'Normally, if we are not out on patrol, we have a game on Saturday afternoons,' Coles said.

'Maybe we can arrange a game, Police versus Army. I will have to Introduce you to Sergeant Hasan, he is a very good player,' said Yilmaz.

'I am sure all the boys will be up for that,' Coles said.

Chief Constable Robin tapped on the shoulder of Yilmaz.

'Are we near there yet, Sergeant?' Robin asked now regretting his decision to join the unit.

Yilmaz pointed to a light.

'That light is coming from the café that is in the centre of the village. The owner has it on all night,' he explained.

Yilmaz retrieved the sheets of paper from his pocket and a self-drawn map of the village with the three houses marked on it. Robin examined it.

'What would you suggest Sergeant?' Robin asked.

'We should split into three groups with each group assigned to one house,' Yilmaz suggested.

'That is the plan I had in my head, so go with it Sergeant,' Robin ordered.

Yilmaz led one group, Sergeant Ali led the second group, and Sergeant Ferdi the third group. Robin decided to join Ferdi's group. Yilmaz and his unit started to jog in the middle of the road until he pointed at the house of one of the terrorist suspects and once the building had been surrounded Yilmaz blew a whistler and soldiers entered through the front and back doors. A man in the house started shouting at the soldiers.

'Where is Michalis?' shouted Yilmaz pointing the gun at the man's face.

'He is not here!' shouted the man.

A few minutes later Yilmaz and the soldiers left the house empty handed and headed to the other houses. Chief Constable Robin and Sergeant Ferdi were standing outside a house.

'What's wrong?' Yilmaz asked.

'They will not open the door,' Ferdi said.

'Who will not?' Yilmaz questioned.

'The occupants,' Ferdi said.

Yilmaz marched up to the front door and raising his leg he kicked down the front door and showed Ferdi the way. The raids proved fruitless as none of the suspects were located. Robin walked up to the angry looking Yilmaz who was sat down by a tree.

'Chin up Sergeant, no luck tonight but never mind we'll get the bastards the next time. I have seen this all before in Kenya and Malay and we find them in the end, but I think the problem will be greater if Britain pulls out. I see the divide between Greeks and Turks growing wider and wider,' said Robin.

'I think you may very well be right sir,' replied Yilmaz.

'Come on Sergeant we have a long walk back.'

The pair joined the other members of the unit on the journey back to the camp.

Considering the unit did not get back to the camp until the early hours of the morning and he had only had four hours sleep, Yilmaz woke up with a spring in his step as he headed to the mess hall, but he was intercepted by one of the men.

'Sir, Inspector Tapping wants to see you in his office.'

Yilmaz knocked on Tapping's office.

'Enter,' said Tapping.

'Take a seat.'

Moments later Sergeants Ali and Ferdi entered and Tapping sat down behind the desk facing the three Sergeants and took a big sigh of breath and looked at the men.

'I regretfully have to inform you all that Sergeant Hasan was shot dead last night in Terra.'

Yilmaz slammed his clinched fist onto Tapping's desk. Tapping stood up.

'Apparently, he was sat outside the café with some friends when a motorbike stopped outside with two men on it and the pillion passenger jumped off ran up to Hasan and shot him at point blank range. I know you were all close to him, especially you, Yilmaz, but I want you to find his killer.'

Yilmaz stood up.

'I am ready to go now.' He stated.

It was midday and the sun and heat were unbearable, but Terra was a hive of activity, not with villagers but with British soldiers and Police, a consequence of the murder of Sergeant Hasan the day before. Yilmaz asked Sulieman to drop him outside his house so he could say a brief hello to Lutfiye and his son. Lutfiye ran over to him and embraced him.

'They shot Hasan,' she said.

'That's why I'm here. How are you doing? You look tired,' he commented.

'I was sick yesterday so your Mother called Doctor Aziz and after he examined me, he said I should go to the hospital in Polis. He said he would call the hospital and make an appointment for Friday morning,' Lutfiye explained.

'What's wrong? Are you ill?'

She smiled at him.

'Dr Aziz thinks I am pregnant.'

'Is he sure?' Yilmaz said breaking out in a huge grin.

'Well, that's why he wants me to go to the hospital for a checkup.'

'Friday. I will ask Tapping if I can have the morning off. I cannot believe it,' said Yilmaz still taking the news in.

'Have you told anyone?'

'No, not until after we have been to the hospital,' she said.

'Where is Zorlu?'

'He is having a nap.'

'Whenever I come round that boy is always sleeping,' he said as he walked into the bedroom to see his son sleeping in their bed.

'I need to go. Did you hear the gunshots yesterday?'

'No, it must have been the time I was being sick. Doctor Aziz was here when Turgut knocked on the door to get the Doctor. He said four shots were fired,' explained Lutfiye.

'I will come back later,' he said as he kissed her and left. Sulieman was still waiting for him in the Land Rover.

'Why are you so happy?' Sulieman asked.

'Just happy to see my wife.'

Four soldiers stood in the road outside the café as Yilmaz and Sulieman arrived. One of the men was Corporal Coles.

'Sergeant I am sorry about your friend.'

'Have you found anything?' asked Yilmaz.

'No, the café owner and the other men are in the café,' Yilmaz walked into the café to find Mustafa, the café owner, Turgut and Salih sat around the table. Yilmaz went round the table embracing each one of the men before sitting down.

'What exactly happened?' Yilmaz asked.

'One minute, let me get you a coffee,' said Mustafa as he got up to make the coffee. 'We were all sat outside drinking coffee. It must have been around five o'clock.'

'Was Hasan wearing his uniform?' Yilmaz asked.

'Yes,' Mustafa confirmed as he bought over Turkish Coffee, three pieces of Turkish Delight and a glass of water on a tray.

'I heard the sound of a motorcycling approaching but did not think anything of it. I saw the bike approaching and I could see two people on it, but again it was nothing unusual. Hasan was too busy talking to take a blind bit of notice of it. The motorcycle slowed down and stopped directly outside. The passenger on the back got off and just walked towards us. All I remember is that he was all in black, black boots, black trousers and a black coat and he was wearing goggles,' Mustafa explained.

'Where was Hasan sat? Yilmaz asked.

'He had his back to the man. I called out "Hasan" and as he turned around the man pulled out a pistol and fired it at Hasan. We all dived to the ground and when I looked up the gunman got on the back of the bike and they made off.'

'What kind of motorcycle was it?'

'I know nothing about motorcycles,' admitted Mustafa.

'Kemal the mechanic does,' interrupted Turgut. 'When I went off to find Doctor Aziz I passed Kemal who was driving a tractor, the motorbike must have gone past him.' The gunman shot him four times. Salih and I tried to stem the flow of blood while Turgut went to find the Doctor,' said Mustafa.

'Has a date for his funeral been set?' asked Yilmaz.

'Not yet,' Salih said.

'I need to go and pay my respects to Fatma,' said Yilmaz standing up. 'I may need to speak to you later,' he shouted out as he left the café. Sulieman was standing by the land rover smoking a cigarette with a British Soldier, but quickly stamped it out before getting in the car.

'Where next?' Sulieman asked.

'I want to go a see Hasan's wife Fatma, but first I want to find Kemal the mechanic.'

They drove to Kemal's garage and Kemal was outside examining under the bonnet of a truck. Yilmaz noticed a couple of motorcycles outside.

'Kemal,' shouted Yilmaz.

This startled Kemal who looked up but failed to recognize Yilmaz, until he walked closer to him.

'Yilmaz, is that you? I didn't recognize you in your uniform.' said Kemal.

'It has been a long time,' Yilmaz said shaking hands with him.

'I presume you are here about Hasan's killing.'

'Yes, did you see the killers on the motorcycle?'

'I did. I was on the tractor when they went past,' confirmed Kemal.

'Can you remember what kind of bike it was?'

'Yes, it was a Norton model 18. Come over here,' Kemal led him to the motorcycles. 'It was a newer version of this bike,' Kemal said pointing to the bike.

'Anything else you can remember?' asked Yilmaz.

'It was moving fast but I am sure the last two numbers of it's registration was 31. Not hundred percent certain and I could not make out the other numbers.'

'Thanks you have been a help.'

Yilmaz rushed back to the land rover and on the car radio he notified the camp with details of the killers' bike.

'Sulieman, let's go to Arodes,'

'Are you sure you want to drive around there in daylight?' questioned Sulieman.

They drove back to the café.

'Corporal!' shouted Yilmaz, 'how would you like to come for a drive to Arodes?

'Why not. Do you have room for one more?' Corporal Coles asked.

'We have space for two in the back,' replied Yilmaz.

'Private Hancock, come with me,' ordered Coles.

The two soldiers got into the back of the Land Rover and they drove off.

'Do you have a lead?' asked the Corporal.

'We have a description of the motorcycle. A Norton model 18 with the registration number ending 31. Shout if you see it! I just have this feeling one of the suspects we were looking for last night in Arodes has something to do with it,' said Yilmaz.

'Did you say your wife is from Arodes?' Corporal Coles asked.

'Yes, she is. The village, just like Terra, is split into two, a Greek part and a Turkish part. Pano Arodes is the Greek part of the village,' explained Yilmaz.

As the Land Rover entered Arodes staring eyes appeared from all directions and soon the vehicle was stuck behind an old tractor and the slow Land Rover became a magnet for a group of youths who started throwing stones at it.

'We need to get past this tractor,' Yilmaz said to Sulieman.

'Hold on,' Sulieman said as he put the vehicle in reverse and sped back to a crossroads before turning off into another road.

'Over there,' Corporal Coles suddenly said pointing towards two parked motorcycles. Sulieman stopped and all four men got out of the vehicle. Even Sulieman carried a sub-machine gun, something he rarely did. The four men started to attract a few bystanders.

'Sergeant Yilmaz, what was the last two digits of that motorcycles registration number?' Private Hancock said raising his hand.

Yilmaz walked towards him.

'31, a Norton Model 18,' Yilmaz shouted.

'I think this could be it, GK4031,' Hancock said.

Sulieman wrote down the number in his notebook.

'Get back in the Rover,' Yilmaz said.

All four men got in and Suleiman drove away.

'Drive round the block and find somewhere to park so we can keep surveillance on the bike,' instructed Yilmaz.

Sulieman drove around until he found a house that had a drive that was covered by grape vines and he reversed in. This was an ideal spot, not only camouflaged from view but it gave protection from the intense bright sun. Suleiman used the Rovers radio transmitter to give details of the motorcycle's registration number. A woman came out from the back door of the house and this prompted Yilmaz to get out of the car and approach her.

'Hello, don't worry we are police, and we need to park in your drive for a while. You can go back into your house.' Yilmaz explained to the woman who rushed back in slamming the door shut.

Suleiman opened the glove compartment and took out a pair of binoculars.

'Can you see the motorbike?' asked Coles and Suleiman put his thumb up.

'We may be waiting for a while,' Yilmaz remarked.

An hour passed and then another and the only activity was a couple of kittens wrestling in the garden.

'I need to go a relive myself,' Hancock suddenly said.

'Find somewhere you cannot be seen,' Coles replied.

Hancock got out the Rover and walked up to higher ground towards fields to the back of the house and stopped when he found a suitable tree he could hide behind. As he finished, he noticed two men walking down the road from behind the houses and quickly rushed back to the Rover.

'There's two men walking this way from the right side,' he told the others.

The two men appeared into view and continued walking towards the two motorcycles.

'Do you think it's them?' asked Coles.

Yilmaz put the strap of his submachine gun around him and opened the car door as the men stopped in front of the motorcycles.

'The second they get on the bikes we rush them,' Yilmaz quietly said, and Coles and Hancock opened their doors and knelt behind them.

The two suspects continued talking and the frustration increased on Yilmaz's face.

'Let's get them,' Coles whispered.

'I want to be certain that the motorbikes belong to them,' Yilmaz whispered back.

The front door of the house opened and the woman who Yilmaz had spoken to earlier came out and started walking towards the two suspects and at this very point Sulieman, looking through the binoculars, saw one of the men take keys out of his jacket pocket and go to mount the bike.

'He has keys,' Suleiman said.

'Go!' shouted Yilmaz and on his comand all four men started to run towards the suspects. The woman started shouting at the suspects.

'What's she doing?' Coles shouted.

'She's warning them,' Yilmaz shouted back.

The two suspects turned to look at the woman and saw the men running towards them and one of the suspects pulled out a pistol from inside his jacket and aimed towards the direction of the woman and pulled the trigger. Yilmaz grabbed the woman and pulled her to the ground out of the way of the gunfire. Coles and Hancock opened fire with their submachine guns, the suspect with the pistol fell to the ground having been shot, and his accomplice dragged him into the front garden of one the houses.

'Sorry about that,' Yilmaz said to woman who lay flat in the middle of the road and spat out a mouthful of dirt. Yilmaz, kneeling on one knee, opened fire at the suspects who were now hid behind a low wooden fence at the side of a house. The woman started swearing at the men in Greek and Sulieman told her to shut up. Yilmaz, Coles, and Hancock ran into garden.

'Cover me,' Coles said as he ran and dived over the fence and Yilmaz and Hancock followed him over the fence, but the two suspects had gone.

'Look here,' Yilmaz pointed to a trail of blood and they followed it to the back of the house, but all they could see where some goats and chickens wandering around the back yard. Coles continued following the trail of blood which stopped in front of the outside toilet. A shot was fired, and Coles slumped to the ground.

'They're in the toilet,' shouted Hancock and he and Yilmaz peppered the wooden toilet door with machine gun fire before Yilmaz kicked in the door to find the two suspects on the floor.

'Sulieman, Sulieman,' yelled Yilmaz at the top of his voice and as Sulieman ran into the yard Yilmaz attended to Coles.

'Sulieman! Radio for assistance, tell them a soldier is down,' ordered Yilmaz.

'Where are you wounded?' asked Yilmaz.

'In my side,' Coles said showing him the blood-soaked shirt.

Yilmaz grabbed a towel from the washing line and placed it over the wound. Hancock stood in the doorway of the toilet, which was just a hole in the ground.

'No movement from these two,' Hancock said.

Yilmaz walked into the toilet and picked up the pistol and threw it outside. One of the men was conscious.

'Did you shoot a Turkish Policeman yesterday?' Yilmaz asked the suspect.

The suspect stared into Yilmaz's eyes and grinned at him.

Units of the police and Fusiliers descended on Arodes. Locals stood around watching, some oblivious to what had happened. Yilmaz and Sulieman were standing in the road next to a military ambulance as Inspector Tapping approached.

'Good work, but next time call for back up. You could easily have been outnumbered. The suspects are two of three men we were looking for last night, they are barely alive, one of them is in a serious condition,' Tapping informed the men.

Yilmaz turned to see Coles being stretchered into the ambulance and he went over to him.

'Corporal, you need to recover as soon as possible so we can play that game of football,' remarked Yilmaz and this put a smile on Cole's face.

'Don't worry I will certainly look you up and arrange a game,' Coles said raising his arm as he was being placed in the back of the ambulance.

A second military ambulance arrived and soon the two suspects were stretchered on both, and strapped into their stretchers.

'Yilmaz, Suleiman, you can escort the ambulance to the hospital in Polis. I'll send relief later,' Tapping ordered.

'Yes, sir,' Yilmaz replied as he and Suleiman returned to the land Rover.

A tractor held up the Land Rover and the ambulance, and Suleiman showed his annoyance by repeatedly pressing the car horn, and the tractor finally moved to the side of the road to allow the vehicles behind to pass.

'Hold on, that's my Father-in-law,' Yilmaz said as he leaned out the window to shout and wave at the tractor driver, who waived back.

'Do you think he recognized you?' Suleiman asked him.

'Probably not.'

Polis General was the second largest hospital in the Western part of the Island, with only Paphos hospital larger. The two wounded suspects were wheeled in through the main entrance, but Yilmaz felt uncomfortable by the number of men who seemed to be loitering outside the entrance. One of the suspects was rushed into theater for an emergency operation, while the other was taken to intensive care. Yilmaz stood guard outside the operating theater whilst Sulieman went to the intensive care unit. An hour passed before the doors to the operating theater swung open and the Doctor walked out, looked at Yilmaz, and shook his head.

'He did not make it,' the Doctor confirmed.

Yilmaz nodded and pushed open the theater doors to see the suspect's covered body on the operating table.

'May I?' Yilmaz asked the Doctor.

'Go ahead, we're finished in there,' the Doctor said as he walked away.

Yilmaz uncovered the face, and he took the sheets of paper with the photos and profiles of the three suspected terrorists. On closer inspection he identified the body as Michalis. Covering the dead man's face Yilmaz left to go to intensive care. Suleiman was asleep on a chair outside the intensive care unit, so Yilmaz kicked his feet to wake him up.

'Oh, what's happened,' a disoriented Suleiman uttered.

'He's dead. It was Michalis,' Yilmaz informed him. 'What about your suspect?'

'No one is saying anything.' Suleiman told him.

Just then Sergeant Ferdi and another Policemen arrived to relieve Yilmaz and Suleiman.

'Yilmaz, Tapping wants to see you,' Ferdi told him.

'What about?' Yilmaz asked bluntly.

'How do I know? Why would he tell me, you are his boy,' came the response from Ferdi heightening the tension in the air.

'You just have to worry about the one in there. The other suspect just died, it was Michalis, Yilmaz said as he and Suleiman walked off. As they left the hospital Yilmaz still seemed concerned about a group of men still standing outside the entrance and the sets of eyes that followed the pair as they walked to their Land Rover.

Tapping was holding a folder of papers when Yilmaz walked in.

'So, the one who died was Michalis. Well done, that is another terrorist off the streets' Tapping said whilst he walked around the room.

Yilmaz stood there for a few silent moments.

'Is that all Sir.'

'No, I have details of your house,' Tapping said as he handed him the folder. 'If you go to the admin department, they will give you the house keys.'

Yilmaz opened the folder and skim read the information.

'Oh, Acting Sergeant, Sergeant Hasan's family have asked if you would be one of the pallbearers at his funeral on Monday.'

'It would be an honour sir.'

'Good I will let them know. Now go and inspect your new house.'

'Thank you, Sir,' Yilmaz said as he walked out with a noticeable spring in his step.

Suleiman and Yilmaz drove round the streets of Polis trying to find Yilmaz's new house.

'Number 20, Salaminos,' said Yilmaz pointing to the address on the sheet.

'I know where it is, it's off Leoforos Mariou,' Suleiman replied as he started laughing.

'What's so funny?'

Sulieman pointed as they drove past a cemetery.

'At least if something happens to you, they don't have far to bury you.'

Yilmaz did not see the funny side of the comment.

'That's where they're holding the funeral for Hasan on Monday,' Yilmaz said in a curt manner.

'Sorry,' Suleiman quietly said.

Finally, they pulled up outside the house and Yilmaz was pleasantly surprised at how nice and smart the front of the house looked. He entered the front door, and this led into a good-sized reception room, and through a sliding door was the lounge. Off the corridor was the bathroom and toilet, two decent sized bedrooms and a large kitchen at the back and a small back yard. Yilmaz did not expect the house to be of this standard, and to think he did not have to pay a penny for the rent. Suleiman had wandered in and was inspecting the rooms.

'Can I have the spare bedroom?' Suleiman said jokingly.

'You can if you don't mind sharing with my two-year-old son.'

'There's a fridge in here,' said Suleiman excitedly. Fridges were a rarity and a luxury in most village houses.

'I cannot wait to show Lutfiye, she'll be amazed,' said Yilmaz.

'When are you going to move in?'

'I have a few days leave from Tuesday so we can move in then.'

Yilmaz closed the front door and took one more lingering look at the house before he and Suleiman left.

Dozens of Fusiliers roamed the streets of Polis. There were two soldiers positioned on every street corner within a one-mile radius of the Mosque. EOKA terrorists had targeted funerals of Turkish Cypriot policemen before so a large military presence was evident on the day of Sergeant Hasan's funeral. The men of the mobile reserve spent the early hours of the morning ironing their uniforms and polishing their boots, belt buckles and jacket buttons. The Sergeants marshalled the unit out of the barracks and onto the parade ground. Tapping stood in front of all the men.

'Today is a tragic day for the Cyprus police force as we bury one of our own men. Sergeant Hasan was one of the most dependable, loyal, and bravest policemen I had the pleasure of working with. Since the beginning of the

Cyprus Emergency, we have lost many good men, and, I will be honest, we may lose more, but the loss of Sergeant Hasan has pained me the most. I have many good memories of him, and I carry these memories for the rest of my days, and I know many of you were close to him, especially the men who came from the same village as the Sergeant. So today we will celebrate his life and give him the most dignified send off we can afford to such a brave man. Can we all give a salute to Sergeant Hasan.' Tapping stood to attention and gave a salute and all the men replicated this. After a minute Tapping lowered his arm.

'All leave has been cancelled until the funeral of Michalis, which will be held in Arodes in five days,' he informed the unit and walked towards the Land Rover and the men marched towards the trucks that would transport them to the funeral. The police unit arrived at the mosque and the men formed a guard of honour except for Sergeants Yilmaz, Ali, Ferdi, and Officer Suleiman, who joined Sergeant Hasan's two brothers to form the six pallbearers. Members of Hasan's family including his wife and three children walked between the guard of honour and entered the mosque. The building was surrounded by British Soldiers, not only a unit of Lancashire Fusiliers but also a unit from the Royal Ulster Rifles. Sergeant Hasan's coffin lay open, his body dressed in his police uniform. The pallbearers stood behind the coffin as mourners filed by. The Imam walked up to the coffin and recited several Islamic prayers, he then gestured for the coffin to be sealed. He then announced that those people who wished to pray make their way to the prayer hall, which had a separated area for women. After the coffin was sealed the Pallbearers lifted the coffin and carried it outside and down the guard of honour, as all the officers gave salute, and placed it on a horse drawn carriage. Family and friends got into cars to follow the carriage to Terra, where Hasan would be buried.

Terra cemetery was on the outskirts of the village and going by the relatively few graves, it had only been built a few years before hand. Four British soldiers circled the perimeter wall of the cemetery as they caught sight of the funeral procession arriving. A soldier stood guard at the cemetery entrance checking the villagers as they entered. The carriage stopped outside, and Hasan's two brothers waited for the others to arrive. The police unit arrived, and Yilmaz, Fedi, Ali and Suleiman joined the brothers in lifting the coffin from the carriage and carrying it into the cemetery, before carefully lowering it into the grave. The officers joined their unit who had lined up behind the Imam. Yilmaz looked towards the group of village mourners that included Lutfiye, his parents and his brother. After the Imam uttered some blessings, the mourners were invited to grab a handful of soil and throw it into the grave onto Hasan's coffin before making their way out of the cemetery. Yilmaz glanced around before breaking rank to join his family.

'Where's Zorlu?' Yilmaz asked Lutfiye.

'My sister is looking after him. Did you get the keys to the house?' She asked him.

'I got them, but they have cancelled my leave until after the funeral of Michalis, so it's going to be next week before we can move in.'

The disappointment was clear on Lutifye's face, but she understood the nature of his job and it would be only another a week before they moved. A few minutes later Yilmaz realized that his unit had left the cemetery and said his farewells before rushing to catch them up.

Tapping was sat in his office going through his paperwork. His administration of his paperwork would be described as basic, he would pick up a folder from the top of his 'to do list' tray review it before putting it back to the bottom of the same tray. His office door was open, and he saw Yilmaz approaching with a folder in his hand and beckoned him in.

'Sir, I have my report of the shooting of Michalis,' Yilmaz said as he placed it on Tapping's desk.

Tapping opened the folder and took a couple of minutes to skim through it.

'Excellent report Acting Sergeant, this is just a formality. I spend more time reading and completing paperwork than my actual job. Now, Michalis' funeral. I want you and Suleiman to go undercover, in civilian clothes, and take photographs of all the mourners who attend to funeral. We know he has links with Grivas so the hierarchy of EOKA may be in attendance. There will be no visible police or military presence, but we will have men disguised on the ground. Oh, apologies for cancelling your leave, but you know how it is Sergeant,' said Tapping has he picked up another file from his to do list.

'I understand Sir.'

It was the day of Michalis' funeral and Suleiman was showing Yilmaz the camera and its telescopic lens. They were both wearing short sleeve shirts and trousers and Yilmaz was carrying a satchel with his pistol in it, Suleiman had his camera in a camera case that he hung around his shoulder. The pair drove to Arodes in an unmarked car and parked it at Yilmaz's father-in-law's house. It was early so they were invited in for breakfast of fried egg and hellim prepared by his mother-in-law, Emine. Yilmaz told them that he would be renting a house in Polis. 'Yilmaz it is dangerous for you but also for Lutfiye and Zorlu, you saw what happened to your friend Hasan,' Emine told him.

Yilmaz had yet to tell anyone that Lutfiye was pregnant.
'I know mother. I try and be as careful as possible and I have Suleiman here to look after me, he said slapping Suleiman on the back.
'He needs looking after,' Suleiman said in a way that made everyone laugh.
Ten minutes was the time it took Yilmaz and Sulieman to walk from the house to the church. A couple of hundred yards from the church was a cluster of trees. Suleiman took up a position in between a pair of trees and nestled in some bushes, camera ready. As villagers began to assemble outside the church Yilmaz mingled with them and soon the hearse, carrying Michalis' coffin arrived. The six pallbearers all dressed in black shirts and black trousers took it out of the hearse and lifted it onto their shoulders. Yilmaz turned to the direction of Suleiman, keen that he took photographs of the six pallbearers. Paying particular attention to the man carrying the coffin at the back Yilmaz opened his satchel and discreetly unfolded the papers and photos of suspected EOKA members he took out the papers but used the satchel as cover in an attempt not to draw attention to himself. He could not be sure if the man was on the list as he was too far away, he slowly walked closer to the church just as the pallbearers carried the coffin into the church and came within a few feet of the pallbearers, he stared at the man at the back and caught his eye. Once the coffin had been carried inside Yilmaz walked towards Suleiman, who had packed his camera in the case. 'The man carrying the coffin at the back I think it's him,' Yilmaz said to Suleiman pointing to one of the photos on the paper.
'Andreou Christos,' uttered Suleiman.
'Do you think it is him?' asked Yilmaz.
'I took a photograph of him, but I can't be sure.'

'Let's go and get the car and radio in,' said Yilmaz as he and Suleiman rushed back to his father-in-law's house. Just over fifteen minutes later Suleiman drove past the church heading to the cemetery before parking nearby. Yilmaz radioed in.

'In position, over and out.'

A good half an hour passed before people began to arrive at the cemetery and ten minutes later the hearse arrived.

'Drive a little bit closer,' Yilmaz told Suleiman.

'I am certain that is Andreou,' said Yilmaz looking at his photo and then observing him carrying the coffin.

Suleiman pointed to a gang of four youths who had been staring at the car and now had decided to walk over.

'Hey,' shouted one of the youths. 'Are you police?'

'Ignore them,' whispered Yilmaz.

'Are you Turks?' 'What are you doing here?' 'Are you spying on the funeral?' The questions came thick and fast.

'Come out the car and speak to us,' one of the youths shouted.

Yilmaz leaned out the passenger side window.

'Boys, go and play with your toys.'

The youths started laughing and one of them ran back to the cemetery. The other three stood in front of the car and one of them started banging on the bonnet. Suleiman turned to Yilmaz who just shrugged his shoulders.

'Oh no,' said Suleiman as the youth ran back out the cemetery followed by several men. Yilmaz took the radio receiver.

'We need to vacate the location, repeat we are vacating the location,' Yilmaz clearly stated.

By now the car was surrounded and then a large stone hit the side of the car. Yilmaz pulled out his pistol from the satchel pointed it outside in the air and fired it. The shot echoed through the village and the men and youths dispersed into all directions.

'We better go,' said Yilmaz tapping Suleiman on the arm. Without hesitation Suleiman turned on the engine and drove off. They only drove a few hundred yards before stopping. Mourners began to trickle out the cemetery entrance, but the mob had seen the car parked further up the road and started walking towards it.

'I think we need to leave, go,' Yilmaz said, and Suleiman performed a swift U-turn and he drove off this time out of the Greek part of the village and into the Turkish area.

'What do we do about Andreou?' asked Suleiman.

'Don't worry we will get him another time. If you process the photographs you took, we will have a photo of him to distribute to the rest of the force,' said Yilmaz. 'Are you free this Sunday?'

'Why? Are you inviting me round for dinner?' Suleiman cheekily said.

'I am sure after you help us move to the new house Lutifiye would prepare you something.'

'What time do you want me there?

'If we leave the camp for Terra at six in the morning we'll be packed and in Polis by lunchtime. My brother is going to take his truck, so he'll take the heavy stuff, so I would be grateful if you could take me, Lutfiye and my son,' explained Yilmaz.

'I will,' confirmed Suleiman.

Sundays in Terra were traditionally family days. Families would normally gather at their parent's house and enjoy a culinary feast. This could consist of lamb shanks cooked over several hours in a outside clay oven or lamb shish barbequed over a coal fire and many vegetable dishes prepared from the produce grown in the village.

Yilmaz and his brother, Isfendiyar, lifted Zorlu's cot onto the truck.

'Are you taking the bed?' asked Isfendiyar.

'No, there is a double bed at the new house, but we need to take the mattress,' said Yilmaz.

Suleiman loaded the back of the Land Rover with luggage packed with clothes. Yilmaz's mother, Fahriye, stood nearby with tearful eyes, wondering to herself now that Yilmaz was moving his young family from Terra to Polis, would he ever return to the village. His Father was against Yilmaz joining the Police force as he wanted his eldest son to work on the farm and the olive groves, but Yilmaz did not want to be a farmer, and even though he was academic his father refused to pay for Yilmaz to continue his education, so after a few years of helping on the farm Yilmaz decided this was not the life for him and signed up to join the police. As the last item was loaded onto the truck Yilmaz walked up to his mother.

'Where's dad?'

'You know him, he is probably on his tractor somewhere,' said his Mum.

'That's typical of him,' remarked Yilmaz.

'Why don't you and Lutfiye stay for lunch and then go.'

'No, we have to unpack and tidy up the new house.'

'You are going to come and visit?' his Mother said with the tears swelling up.

'Of course, we are going to come and visit, Zorlu is not going to forget his grandparents.'

They embraced and she went over to say goodbye to Lutfiye and Zorlu. Yilmaz looked through the house one last time.

'We are ready to go,' he declared.

Lutfiye said her goodbyes and she and Zorlu got into the back of the Land Rover.

'Isfendiyar, follow us.' Shouted Yilmaz as he got into the front passenger's seat.

'Let's go Suleiman,' instructed Yilmaz.

The Land Rover and truck headed off as the vehicles departed the village, Yilmaz put his head out the car door window and wondered what future lay ahead for him and his family and whether he would ever return to Terra.

Printed in Great Britain
by Amazon